BODIES FULL OF BURNING

An Anthology of Menopause-Themed Horror

Edited by Nicole M. Wolverton

D1521798

All rights reserved. No part of this publication may be reproduced, stored in or introduced into a retrieval system, or transmitted in any form, or by any means (electronic, mechanical, photocopying, recording or otherwise) without the prior permission of the publisher. Any person who does any unauthorised act in relation to this publication may be liable to criminal prosecution and civil claims for damages.

The following is a work of fiction; names, characters, businesses, places, events and incidents are fictitious. Any similarities to actual persons living or dead, events, places and locations is purely coincidental.

This edition first published 2021 – also available as an ebook

Paperback ISBN: 9798536828199

© 2021 Sliced Up Press.

Web: sliceduppress.com / Twitter: @sliceduppress

Blood Calumny © Joe Koch, *It Will Have Blood, They Say* © Marsheila Rockwell, *The Sound of Snow and Cacti* © Monique Quintana, *Here There Are Dragons* © Megan M. Davies-Ostrom, *Four Acres and a Shovel* © Carman Webb, *Nobody Warns You* © D.A. Jobe, *In Bloom* © Dr Bunny McFadden, *Transcending* © Julie Ann Rees, *Inferno* © Victory Witherkeigh, *Fledglings/Crones* © B.J. Thrower and Karen Thrower, *Trouble in Room Eight* © E.F. Schraeder, *Ole Higue* © Jennifer D. Adams, *Becoming* © Ali Seay, *Some Say the World Will End in Fire* © Jude Reid, *Fifty-Four Year Itch* © Shelby Dollar, *This is Yours* © Max Turner

CONTENTS

Editor's Introduction

It's always about blood, it seems. Everything to do with ovaries and uteruses (and their byproducts) is fraught in some way, whether you own them or used to own them or are supposed to own them or perhaps were never really meant to own them. Horror fiction on the page and on the screen abounds when it comes to puberty and the arrival of the menstrual flow — I know very few people who haven't read or seen Stephen King's *Carrie*. But when it comes to menopause and what happens when the blood dries up, the literary and cinematic horror landscapes are fairly barren (pun intended).

Bodies Full of Burning erupted out of a Twitter yearning of mine to see some menopause-themed horror fiction (since, at nearly fifty years old, I'm in the throes of perimenopause myself and often joke about how when my first hot flash hit — on an international solo trip and in public — I seriously considered whether I'd been possessed, had accidentally died and gone straight to Hell, or was on the verge of spontaneously combusting to ash). The very wonderful owner of Sliced Up Press popped up and said, "yes, definitely, let's do this."

To say that the idea of an anthology like *Bodies Full of Burning* sparked some conversations in the horror community — and outside of it — is an understatement. And what became clear while reading the submissions and talking to writers is that people need an outlet for the full range of their lived experiences and fears when it comes to menopause. Horror writing is a natural fit. But don't go thinking that all the stories are doom, gloom, and terrifying awfulness — transitions can be empowering, too, which is also reflected in *Bodies Full of Burning*.

So. Thanks to Sliced Up Press for the opportunity to curate this fantastic anthology. Thanks to the seventeen writers whose stories make up the collection. Thanks to the many more writers who submitted stories that were so great I lost sleep over making decisions. And, of course, thanks to the horror community for their genuine excitement and support. I hope all of you find something to love, fear, and have nightmares about within these pages.

Sliced Up Press is releasing this anthology in September in honor of National Menopause Awareness Month in the U.S. and in anticipation of World Menopause Month in October.

Best wishes,
Nicole M. Wolverton

BLOOD CALUMNY
Joe Koch

Kevin didn't want to share a room with their mother. In the tiny house after the divorce, she said they didn't have a choice. Telling this to Bastien while lighting a cigarette to appear casual, because their hands and mouth need something to do in the huge chasm between speaking and waiting to be judged, need anything other than Bastien's hurt silence, Bastien's head turning away; Kevin insists it's nothing personal. "It's not you, it's me. I can't be with anyone. Not like this."

Alone again, because it's what they asked for — now isn't it? Kevin crushes what's left of their cigarette, dumps the contents of the ashtray in the outdoor bin, and washes their hands longer than they really need to. Puts the ashtray in the nightstand drawer with the remnants of a pack of cigarettes, a bad brand and a bad habit from college that Kevin gave up years ago.

They're not responsible for what it does though, either, because it's not their choice, it never has been, and if Bastien or anyone else could understand — but they can't. The blood, the tears, the murders — and now that Kevin's older, the heat, the rage, the unpredictable eruptions that never came like clockwork and come now hard with increasing frequency and capricious vengeance against the host. The parasite people call a blessing.

It's not like Kevin hasn't tried to have it taken out.

Planned Parenthood in 1987, University Women's Center in 1992, Ladies First Fem-Care in '99, Planned Parenthood again in '01, Sweet Valley Whole Woman's Health in 2010, and on and on for nearly fifty years, a litany of providers saying dear and hon and Miss Kevin, reciting a litany of excuses with clucking tongues. It doesn't matter if Kevin's a big, hairy guy waving money in their faces and begging them to get the monster out. The minute Kevin hits an exam table, the clucking starts.

Left to take matters into their own hands, Kevin closes the tobacco drawer in the nightstand. Modelled on an apothecary cabinet with eight stacked compartments, it hides a hatch holding errata shipped across the country after their father died. Masculine objects recall life before the onset: coins, pocketknives, a rusted harmonica, marbles, an old watch. Kevin decides on a military folding knife with a three-and-a-half-inch blade. Opens the knife and places it next to their phone charger in easy reach.

In the tiny house, after the divorce, sharing a room with mom because the girls were older, the girls deserved privacy, Kevin's arguments dismissed as selfish. Kevin can't sleep. Not with their mother fighting off blankets like an invisible assailant. The house asleep, the world asleep, their mother unconscious, Kevin cornered in the extra bed between

11

the thrashing woman and the bedroom door. Her sleeping body kicks and flails. Face flops over in Kevin's direction, pouring sweat. A smile crawls onto her slack lips. Mouth emits a pleasured moan. There's a smell of rotten musk; something meaty and slippery releases itself from tangled legs and sheets. Wet noises slop out, and a limping shadow skulks away, wandering the walls and ceiling in the darkness. Kevin freezes, stares, tracks its progress. Lumbering like a giant slug, thick and moist, it blends into the rustling curtains and merges with tossed blankets. It unfurls in recessed corners where the moonlight can't reach. Dangles for an hour above Kevin's toy chest; sways like an extra appendage from the ceiling lamp. Swims through pools of shadow poured between furniture and floor. Finally prowling to the foot of their mother's bed, turning in circles like an angry cat, it wiggles beneath the disordered covers and squeezes back into its hiding place with a loud pop.

In the morning, Kevin's mother tries to hide the stain. Don't be scared. I'm going through the change. Someday you'll understand.

Sometimes in the suppurating night-time shadows, it gets lost. Meandering senile, perched atop a tall dresser next to their mother's handbag, working its two thick, prehensile loops around to imitate the shape. Thudding on the floor and lying immobile for hours as if drunk. Kevin can't hide in the bathroom or stay awake all night watching the wandering lump of shiny musculature with its trailing webs of fat. Sooner or later, Kevin has to sleep.

One night they wake up in the dark. Their mother snores. Stuffed animals guard the L-shaped

12

perimeter of Kevin's cramped bed. Kevin reaches for the safety of a favorite plush elephant, its floppy ears deformed by moonlight. The soft, furry body presses against Kevin's chest, but the trunk is slick, wet, and smelly. Kevin doesn't remember dropping the toy in the toilet or having an accident.

When they understand what their senses are saying, it's too late to throw the thing against the wall and escape its embrace.

If Kevin tried to explain the invasion to Bastien, imagine the derision. You're not telling me you really believe that, are you? All kids have bad dreams. Yes, Kevin would have to confirm. That is exactly what I believe. And then Kevin would have to talk about the murders.

Because it's never been enough for the parasite to co-opt a habitat inside Kevin's body, first snip, snip, snipping away at the natural epithelial barrier, then ballooning inward with murderous suction, and last looping its flexible appended egg sacs through painful ligatures, stringing bubble-soft proliferations within the cradle of Kevin's bones. Kevin's mother exhausted as a host, the parasite throbbing with new life. Kevin clotted with abdominal gristle as it spits irregular blood. Wandering still, it comes back sated with strange blood; black, brown, elastic, and stringy; smelling of foreign anatomies; pitted with liverish clumps. What it kills, Kevin never questions. It moves like a thief. Kevin catches it with the knife.

Marks on the nightstand, the mattress, the hardwood floor: failed impalements. Kevin feels it fighting dormancy as they age, yet still it weighs heavy, holding on inside them between erratic manic travels and explosive gore. Gone for days, maybe a whole week now, and god knows Bastien can't be allowed to stay over, can't be the next witness or victim; Kevin waits alone, armed as the sun goes down, pretending to sleep. A shadow in the dark, a lump in the sheets. All the reasons Kevin never lets a lover spend the night.

It rears. Kevin strikes.

Try explaining the knife to Bastien, the cries of the thing strong and unruly after a bloody jaunt. Insistent on its territorial claim to Kevin, it wrestles with smooth muscle and fallopian fists though stabbed and blubbering. If it squealed madly, Kevin might have the guts to kill it. Instead, pinned on the nightstand, slickly twisting, globs of empathic fat flinging, it weeps. Coagulates of mourning, choruses of outrage for the loud injustices against those who bear it, the parasite pleads for the oneness of mercy.

Did she know?

Kevin wonders, and doubt destroys resolve. Litanies of maybe, of anti-abraxas, of Hecate burning. Earthly trinities work their binding legacy upon Kevin's unquiet rebellion, begging acceptance. The subtle ache and absence. The horror cloying, wet, and warm. The spongy egg sacs sticking to Kevin's wrist, parasite climbing their arm, ripping open as it pulls free of the severing blade. Escapes the knife with its fundus spliced.

It sticks, and Kevin can't resist. Piercing like a mole, it spreads where Kevin is tender, working them apart. It lingers with maternal affinity. That in which Kevin gestated now gestates angrily inside them.

14

Kevin coughs up a clot of blonde hair in the kitchen sink. They know better than to risk the bathroom where the mirror reflects a true crime line up of lost lives. A dead-naming phlebotomist. A cop minimizing a threat. Store clerks saying ma'am. Strangers telling them to smile. Vengeance perpetrated against ignorant offenders, inconsistent visions shared by the parasite in its homing state, dreaming as Kevin vomits guilt like a reluctant, unborn twin.

Worst are the unknown trolls, the faces Kevin can't recognize, for unlike the foreign thing that hunts and comes back to nest in their body, Kevin can't read thoughts. They've cancelled all their social accounts. They plug their ears when gossip starts. Kevin can't carry the burden of the parasite's reprisals. They curse the media for broadcasting the personal opinions of the rich and famous, for encouraging discourse as if embedded bias was up for debate. Every keyword blocked, news seeps through.

Kevin agrees with the parasite that hatred is not negotiable. The sight of the beloved icon's face bloated in strangulation, hair swathed around the neck and laced over the eyes like a perverse wedding veil, her swollen tongue popping through the long, blonde gauze, its red tip turning grey; the outcry of fans in grief and shock; it's too much for Kevin to bear.

9-1-1 to report a crime. Alone in the dark, the shadow lump listening inside, oh god, it knows, please hurry; Kevin waits for a call back. A sarcastic operator, another transferred call. After midnight, with instructions to stay home, they wait for the detective to follow up. Hours later, a ringtone Kevin hardly recognizes. A deep, weary monotone.

So your uterus wanders —
Not mine. Hers. My mother.
Okay, so your mother's uterus wanders around killing people.
Yes.
But it lives inside you.
Yes.
And it's happened before. The killing.
Well, yes.
And you didn't do anything to stop it?
You don't understand. I —
We have a witness that places you in your home on the night in question at ten. How did you cross the Atlantic so fast?
I told you, it's not me —
Oh right, right. So your little friend did it.
If you insist on calling it that.
Sorry, your mother's little friend. Did it sprout little wings?
I — I just want it to stop.
Let me give you a bit of advice. My wife is about your age and she —

Kevin fumbles and hangs up.

The creature stirs. Morning's half-light quiets its rumblings, but there's no doubt the tenor of Kevin's restless night has renewed the prospective hit list. Half the local police force, Kevin frets, trying their best not to wish ill on the patronizing bastards, trying not to fuel the fire with vengeful thoughts. Perhaps the parasite wants nothing more than respect,

16

like an old person sent out to pasture. It's old, at least twice as old as Kevin, and who knows how old it was before it made its way into their mother's mind, body, life.

Did she know?

Kevin hunts for clues in her curse: Someday you'll understand.

In response, the restless, kindred organ stretches its misplaced muscles, releasing a fast, unexpected river of blood that shoots down Kevin's leg. Pooled in their shoe, streaked on pants and bedding, splattered on the floor all the way to the bathroom in lavish drops. A bristling sensation of needles feeds on their skin. If Kevin questions how much their mother loved them, they dismiss the obvious answer in a heated decision during clean-up.

Quick, on the phone, before they lose their nerve: "I've been thinking it over. What you said about moving forward."

Bastien, wary as hell: "What happened last night? The fucking police called."

"The thing is this. I think you're right. It's time I quit running away from commitment."

"You do? Why now?"

Kevin, biting their lip. If there were any other way — but Kevin's done their time serving the unwanted inheritance. Bastien is young enough to handle the legacy, young enough to fight off public calumny, a generation younger than Kevin and reared on social justice. Bastien doesn't have murderous thoughts like Kevin, and if they find out no one can kill it —

Kevin says, "Do you want to come over and

spend the night?"

IT WILL HAVE BLOOD, THEY SAY
Marsheila Rockwell

She never bathed in blood. Oh, I know that's what the stories say, but there was never any proof of it, was there? Just rumors and salaciousness, sensationalism and lies. The same things that bring down strong women who refuse to be cowed, even to this day.

Did she torture servants, peasants, even the daughters of lesser gentry sent to her to learn how to be ladies? Or did she try to strengthen and harden them against a world that would visit far worse indignities upon them than anything they might suffer at her hand? Some might argue the subject is open for debate.

Was she a serial killer? Remember, it was the tail end of the Middle Ages in what was even then a backwater country. And women have always been disposable, their disappearances only notable if they are rich, or white, or preferably both. Don't believe me? Look up "Missing and Murdered Indigenous Women and Girls" sometime and then get back to me on that, hmm?

Of course I'm just being rhetorical. My point is, a lot of girls died back then, for a lot of reasons, and blaming those deaths on a woman who was becoming too powerful for the comfort of the local patriarchy was … awfully convenient, wasn't it?

Don't get me wrong. I'm no Báthory apologist. I'm just a middle-aged archaeologist and historian who has, until recently, been excavating the grounds of Castle Csejte in Slovakia, hoping to learn the truth of the Countess' story. Because unlike people with their myriad murky motivations, bones and stones do not lie.

Did you know there was supposedly a book? A diary, that Jakab Szilvássy purportedly saw, detailing Erzsébet's many crimes. Conveniently numbering them, a grand total of 650 — a nice, round figure, easy to remember when you're rehearsing lines. Curiously, Jakab never mentioned said book in his testimony during her trial. If it truly were an accounting of her evil deeds, written in her own hand (in virgin's blood, no doubt), it would have been an open and shut case, no? So why not introduce it into evidence?

Because it didn't actually exist? It would have been profoundly stupid for Erzsébet to keep a record of her victims, and she was demonstrably not a stupid woman. She was known to be one of the most educated women of her time, adeptly managing the business affairs of the estates and villages under her husband's care while he was away at war.

Or was it because the book was exculpatory? That seems far more likely, doesn't it?

Well, we'll soon know the answer, one way or the other.

Because I found it.

***

[Translated from Hungarian]

Ferenc, my Black Knight of Hungary, has returned, but, as ever, it is only for a short time. His duties at the front keep us apart too often and too long, and I miss his warmth in my bed. But even that pleasure is denied us, for though he is ready and I am willing, my body does not cooperate as it did in my youth; my purse remains dry, rendering his affection painful and unsatisfactory for us both.

***

Doesn't sound much like a serial killer's diary, does it? (Granted, there is often a sexual component to serial murder, but that's rape, not intercourse. It's about power, not pleasure.)

This entry isn't dated — most of them aren't — but Erzsébet's husband, Count Ferenc Nádasdy, is known to have fought in the Long War from 1578 until his death in 1604. Erzsébet was born in 1560; she would have only been fifty-four when Ferenc died. However, the Count was also known to have suffered from some unidentified illness that caused debilitating pain in his legs. The onset of that illness was sometime in 1601, and it is unlikely he would have been in any shape to leave deposits in Erzsébet's "purse" after that.

So this entry logically predates 1601, when Erzsébet would have been fifty-one. Today, accepted wisdom is that menopause begins for most women

21

around the age of fifty — that's when it started for me, sadly — but it's believed that the average age has risen over the years, and of course every woman's journey is different.

However, her last child was born in 1598, so it seems likely that, for Erzsébet, "The Change" and its attendant symptoms — like the vaginal dryness referred to in this entry — occurred between 1598 and 1601. Interestingly, while a few rumors of The Blood Countess' depravities appear earlier than that, the majority of them date to this time period.

Coincidence?

***

Katarína found me crying today after Ferenc left. I do not know why I confided in her — she is a sweet enough child, but far below my station, and no fitting confidante, but must needs, I suppose.

She told me my malady was not uncommon, that many women suffer from it, low and highborn alike. She also said she had heard of an old folk cure, but she was not sure I would have the stomach for it.

I saw the disappointment on Ferenc's face when he left my bedchamber, and I know what it portends.

I will have the stomach for it.

***

Interesting, no? Katarína Benická was one of four servants accused with Erzsébet. While the other three servants were executed in gruesome Middle Age fashion, Katarína was merely sentenced to life imprisonment, as she was believed to have acted only under the domination of the other women.

An innocent forced to go along with the others, or a masterful manipulator who avoided almost certain death by playing the victim? Perhaps Erzsébet can shed some light.

***

Ferenc left scant hours ago, and I am compelled to write down what happened between us, lest I forget and lose my nerve when next he visits.

Two days ago, I received word that Ferenc was to return, so I summoned Katarína and demanded the cure. She told me she would bring it to me that evening, before his arrival, but that I must prepare myself to receive it, bathing in milk under the light of the moon.

Fearing some witchcraft, I almost relented, but my desire to be with my husband won out over my Christian guilt. After dinner, I had the other girls fill my bath with fresh milk and help me remove my dress, then bid them depart as I drew the curtains open to let in the moonlight and stepped naked into the tub.

The milk was icy as fresh-melted snow and caused gooseflesh to ripple across my skin as I submerged myself. When I resurfaced, Katarína was there, carrying a small, limp hare, a sack, a bucket, and a knife.

She told me to leave the bath and go to my bedchamber, arranging myself on the bed with my legs splayed wide. Once again, I nearly put a stop to

23

the proceedings, but a commotion at the gate let me know that Ferenc had arrived and I was out of time.

Urging her to hurry, I did as she bade, feeling strangely aroused both by my nakedness and by my wanton position. That feeling vanished as I watched Katarína, standing at the foot of the bed, slice the hare's throat, catching its blood in the bucket. Then, before I could fathom her awful intent, she dropped the hare's carcass in the sack, dipped her hand into its blood, and darted forward, driving questing fingers deep inside my womanhood as she muttered words I could not quite make out.

I tried to recoil, but she commanded me to be still, and I obeyed. I felt her coating my sheath, not ungently, with the animal's warm, thick blood, and the feeling of arousal began to reawaken.

But then she removed her hand, quickly gathered up her things, and withdrew. As she departed, I saw her licking her fingers.

Moments later, Ferenc entered, and, seeing me laid out so shamelessly before him, hurriedly stripped off his clothing and joined me, his manhood soon driving into me, far less gently than Katarína's fingers had done.

Ferenc, well-pleased at the changes encountered, was quickly ready for more, but alas, the hare's blood could no longer oblige, and he left soon after, that look of disappointment having returned.

That look auguring he would soon grow tired of my debility and seek out others with beds more accommodating than my own if it were not cured.

When he had gone, Katarína reemerged.

She told me that a small animal's blood would

only last a short time. If I wanted to continue to please my husband, whenever he wanted, for as long as he wanted, I would need something ... bigger.

Knowing that I stood upon the edge of a dangerous precipice, nevertheless I nodded, and told her to do what must be done. The sight of the bloody smile she wore as she turned away will forever haunt me.

***

Ah, now we get to the crux of it. There *was* a bath, and there was blood, but it wasn't what the legends say it was. It seldom is.

Still, it's easy to see how this must have played out, isn't it? Desperate to keep her husband, Erzsébet — her actions aided and abetted, if not completely governed, by the witch Katarína — would have progressed to larger and more frequent sacrifices. Katarína would have chosen them — it's unlikely Countess Báthory would have gone among the peasantry, hand-picking those whose blood would soon become the 16th century's version of lube.

It's also unlikely there were anywhere near the 650 victims cited, unless Erzsébet was bedding every able-bodied male within a fifty-mile radius of Castle Csejte while her beloved Ferenc was away. History is written by the patriarchy, of course, so a woman in Erzsébet's time who enjoyed sex and wasn't particular about who she enjoyed it with would no doubt have been labelled a monster, and a multitude of sins — hers or otherwise — heaped upon her doorstep.

25

Come to think of it, that's pretty much how women who enjoy sex and aren't shy about it are treated today — though, admittedly, slut-shaming doesn't generally involve accusations of serial murder.

But Erzsébet doesn't really present as a repressed nympho who'd just been sitting around waiting for some supernatural excuse to let her freak flag fly, does she? By her own account, she only did what she did because she was afraid her husband would stray. And while infidelity was an accepted indiscretion among the nobility in that day and age, it did not appear to be the norm in her relationship with Ferenc.

Let's return to the diary, shall we? There are no doubt many answers within it still waiting to be uncovered.

***

Ferenc's arrivals have become less predictable, often unannounced. I have moved my bedchamber; Katarína now sleeps in the room adjacent to mine, so that she may be always ready with the blood whenever my Count should come to collect his husbandly due.

I have forbidden her from killing them in front of me. Their blood is already on my hands, and I am daily wracked with guilt; their deaths need not also bedevil my dreams.

I might have ended this whole affair long ago, even though it meant giving up Ferenc's embrace forever, save for the fact that I was finally able to

26

make out the words of Katarína's spell, and I know now that I am already damned for all eternity.

She spake thusly:

A bath of milk to stoke desire
Quenched only by the Lord of Fire
As this blood flows in place of quim
The soul thus slain belongs to him

I will not see my husband again after this life is done, for he, a good Christian, will enter into Heaven, while I, in league with a witch, am condemned to attend Satan's every whim. So I must make the most of every moment I have with my dear Black Knight while I still can, and I will use any means at my disposal to ensure those moments are as frequent and last as long as possible.

I pray those poor young women can forgive me, for I know God never will.

***

Well, there it is. She *was* a killer, after all, if only by proxy. But perhaps she can be forgiven for entering into an infernal bargain, the terms of which were not revealed until it was far too late. After all, she did it for love, that noblest of motives. That should count for something, no?

You disagree? Love is why I brought you here, you know. Oh, not because I love *you*, of course — I don't have any feelings about you one way or the other. This isn't personal. You're just a target of convenience, living a high-risk lifestyle, whose

27

disappearance isn't likely to draw much — if any — attention.

No, because, like poor Erzsébet, I love my husband, and I want to keep him around. Middle age is when they start looking at themselves — and you — and thinking they can do better. Menopause is definitely a check in the "con" column when they start weighing their options — who wants to constantly be stopping and grabbing at the lube in the middle of sex because your wife's head is into it but her pussy isn't? Talk about a turn-off! It's worse than waiting for his little blue pill to kick in.

Unlike poor Erzsébet, I know exactly what the terms of the bargain I'm about to enter are, and I'm more than happy to sign on the dotted line. That's why I went to the castle in the first place, actually. The stories about her supposedly bathing in blood always made me wonder; I knew there were spells out there that could do what I wanted, and I knew bathing was a key component. But I could never quite put all the pieces together until I found her diary. It was very thoughtful of her to include the proper incantation.

Enough talking. The milk is getting warm; we need to wrap this up so I have time to get ready. My husband will be home soon, you see, and this is the perfect opportunity to test Katarína's spell.

It's date night.

THE SOUND OF SNOW AND CACTI
Monique Quintana

Pale things and robots were slowly taking over our town, and Macrina Lopez was changing again. The bots needed a place to live, and they began to rent the apartments over the laundry mat. One morning while I was pulling red planting pots for our front door at Macrina's store, I saw the bots walk by through the wooden slats on the lattice, their yellow eyes staring at me. Laughing, I heard them call me a fool and mimic my mother's snicker. Like Macrina, my mother was changing, too. At night they whispered to cacti. *We need to change so that this town will be ours again.*

We all knew my kid sister's boyfriend was a monster of bots. He envied that empty lot in our town, the one that you could see if you looked over the bridge from the freeway. Then the first time he came to town, he choked on the hot, dusty air. For us, breathing comes easier than that. The plan for the empty lot was to build a box hardware store with a gardening section. You see, that wouldn't work for us because we already had everything we needed. Our hardware shop had a greenhouse run by one of the most respected women in town, Macrina. She

29

managed the key counter and gave popcorn to all the little girls that came in with their fathers. Everybody's favorite time of year was Christmas, when the family hung wreaths over the werewolf heads leftover from Halloween. Once I had imagined a head was one of the Mexican wolf boys, celebrities that I fantasized would take me away from the town and show me how to love like a circus woman. He'd bite my mouth so hard that I would be joyful for eternity, and no physical pain would faze me. A headache in the eye socket, sore throats in tropical weather would be nothing. Love and riches could snuff out the burns from the kitchen comal that we got every morning.

Before Chris came to town, I didn't appreciate what I had, and I sure as heck didn't understand my family. The morning he showed up for breakfast with my sister, I had gotten into an argument with my mother about a puffy cloud that had shown up in my X-ray on a recent doctor's visit. She was angry that I showed up at the doctor's office in fishnets and a blue patent leather skirt that made the receptionist blush. She had heard about it all from the women in town, how I had shown up looking like I was going to the club. Stacking pears and strawberries in a glass bowl, I tried to silence out my mother's words, but my chest began to hurt so hard that I placed my hand over my heart, my first time doing so because I've always hated the Pledge of Allegiance at school. I told her I'd get the spot checked out at a doctor's office in the city, the one that she had recommended after thumbing through the yellow page books that we used as doorstops when we hung clothes out on the line at night.

I'll never forget the way that motherfucker hummed. Chris, I mean. Later that night, my mom said that he had a lot of nerve to show up to our house in shorts when she made all three of my brothers cover their legs and wear shirts with collars and sleeves. Our father had been dead too long to help my mother, but she still spoke to him often when the sun went down, cursing him for making us such stubborn children. My mother grew more powerful every day.

My mother said to set the table like bones. Even though it was late in the morning, there was a pale pink clearing in the sky, like it didn't want to let us start our meal or a visit. We disobeyed the sky then because we loved my little sister. When she was born, I was not too fond of the poor thing because my family praised her for her pale skin. When she first learned to crawl, I caught her playing with knives on the kitchen floor, banging the blades on stainless steel pots like a drum. I ran to my mom, hush-screaming in my palms like praying for death to take us all. My mother crept behind my sister and pulled the knives from her dimpled hands, soft like dove feathers. I thought Miranda was dead that day, but she had lived miraculously to make it to this sacred meal. And now she had Chris, and no one needed to say anything except sigh into the drywall of our house. He was something we knew was coming.

On our dining table, he rolled out the blueprints for Sparky's, the long roll of paper making a shattering sound on the table. That's what he wanted to bring to our city — a home improvement warehouse with lumber and electrical lights. There would be patio furniture and plastic lawn flamingos, and mini retro refrigerators that ladies could put their cold cream and Korean face masks into. The building would go up fast. I heard one of my brothers swallow his wine with a thud at the prospect. Chris said he could erect the building in a matter of days. My mother snickered, as she always does in the morning. *How would this be possible?* she asked, her voice pricked not with wonderment but with condescension. We had many encounters with businesspeople, with men from affluent families, but none outside our town. We wondered why the universe thought we had to oblige this man, especially as our winter was drawing near. It was our favorite season for the long nights. As a family, we knew that we could kill each other if the days were too long.

But it was possible to build Sparky's that quick. He'd have it open just in time for the Christmas shopping season. He had done such projects before. He looked to Miranda to give the nod in agreement, but instead she smiled at me and took me by the wrist. Everything will be just fine, I know it, she said. My fork dropped under the table, and I leaped to get it, searching the man's shoes for evidence of chicken feet. That was the sign of the devil. I found nothing of the sort and had to tell myself he was harmless.

He brought in his father's company to lay everything down, and the building went up faster than it took for the fog to come from the ocean we had never seen before. We waited for "Help Wanted" signs or job announcements in the local newspaper, but they never came. I asked Miranda about this as I saw her coming from my mother's bedroom one day carrying a pot of soup. As I walked close to her, I could see the old amber in her eye. The color that I had also envied when she was a little girl. Any man was undeserving of her. I knew she was as kind as she had always been. I could feel the chicken bones stand up in the pot. What is Chris doing? I thought he was going to hire our people to run the store, I told her. I could hear my mother moaning in the room from her ailments. The carrots scorched on the bottom of the pot. Miranda laughed and reassured me that everything would work out just fine. She handed me the pot. *Here, the rest is for you.* Our mother was changing every day.

The mist clung to the window as I ate the soup. For the first time in years, I was grateful to be back in that house with my mother. For the longest time, I had hated every part of it. The bricks that swayed to the left in the summer. There was the outdated wallpaper with brown flowers bent over as if they were pleading for me to love them. As I looked out the window, I could see the warehouse roof, with birds appearing to float and peck at the dust in the fog. The lights flickered too fast on their beaks for me to make out what kind of birds they were, but they walked stiffly, their throaty call like honey. I snapped the bones in my bowl and ate the soft parts inside.

The scent of wood is unforgivable. He brought in robots from the city to be the automatic checkers. Their heads donned hats, and their digital stomachs would display what each customer owed them for things they could already get at Macrina's store. Our townspeople would never give this new place business, Macrina said. But it didn't matter. People began to ride into Sparky's from the freeway in their high-rise pick-up trucks, hollering at the sunshine and catcalling our women as they walked home from the grocery store with their bags of vegetables.

I felt as if I would weep when I began to see our people shopping at Sparky's. I even took to standing outside of the store and mad dogging them when they went inside. Macrina told me to pay them no mind. She told me there would always be such lost ones, so far away from the cacti flower that they would never know how to smell it again. I sat with her at her key counter, and she poured me chocolate in a clay cup from a coffee pot. The chocolate tasted like the coffee, bits of the grind scratching my throat. There had been other worries. The bots were trying to buy property in town, even setting down money for burial plots in our cemetery. *Why would they need burial plots?* I asked. Macrina was carving a snake from the step of a thick plant that she had taken from the garden. The pink flower in the plant began to make my eyes itch. Everyone has their rituals, the things they want to bury, she told me. The green from the plant made me think of my sister. One winter, when she still lived at home, she went months wearing the same green sweater every day. She wore it so much that there was a hole near her stomach where she rubbed incessantly. Like me, she complained of the burn there.

We waited until morning time to see the bots. Macrina wore the best dress from her closet, a red velvet dress over a pair of pants that flapped at her ankles in the wind. Miranda, my sister, wore a white muslin, a dress that never was, a dress she would have sewed in the wrong way if she had the opportunity. It

34

was her angelic thing, the prayer against the thing that took her from home in the first place. She would make her first dead there in the fall of lumber. Her pale man was the first to go. We let her do the ritual. The heart's shape makes pleasing shapes in sawdust, the new moaning that my sister would hear and never hear again in an instant. We could see the bots coming for us, running as if their god made their arms from the air. Cans sprayed us colorless, the chemicals masking our eyes through our breathing, the choking, and the pain from our breasts and our stomachs. Our thick bodies made their pound of the pavement. Drilling bot eyes, bot limbs, blue shocking out like the motors that ran across the highway above us. All those tin cars and people not getting off the exit ramp did not choose to pass through our town. Macrina's hair was coming out of her braid until a snow of blood made it mat to her head.

The ceiling fans like birds chirping, chirping a sound of ritual. The slabs of the artificial light swung over us, yellow, making a bleating sound. Crush the bot eyes until they don't come here anymore. In the bots, we ripped the skin, bleeding. Blood came from all of the orifices of the bots. Chemical and mist from a white ocean we had never seen before, that we would never wish to see. No snow comes here, and it never will again. Macrina screamed so hard in their mouths that we knew we would hear about this day for the rest of our lives. We'd eat our cactus blooms from blue bowls for breakfast.

HERE THERE ARE DRAGONS
Megan M. Davies-Ostrom

My name is Yanna, and I'm fifty-one years old. I've been a warrior, a hunter, a wife, a mother, and a grandmother. Fifty-one good years. But my monthly blood stopped flowing a year ago, and now it's my turn to feed the dragons.

I grip my spear and stare into the shadowed halls beneath the tall and ancient trees. Darker, older, wilder; we do not hunt in these woods. We do not cut trees or harvest berries and roots here. Those who tried have never returned. My hands don't tremble, and for that I am glad. My mother and grandmother went into the Winter Woods tall, straight, and proud when their times came, and I would do the same.

Everyone is watching from the walls. Young and old, weak and hale, the entire community has gathered, from the frailest, teetering grandfather to the tiniest babe-in-arms. My husband, daughters, and little granddaughter are there too. I hugged them goodbye when I passed the gate; held them tight and whispered love to tear-streaked faces. I remember how much it hurt when my own mother walked through the gate. Losing her cut a piece from my heart. I missed her guidance, her strength, and the way

36

her smile filled her eyes with laughter. It will be the same for them. Missing our mothers is the price we all pay for safety.

As I left, I pressed my favorite bow into my granddaughter's hands. A good weapon; it will suit her well when she's grown, and I have no use for it where I'm going. Arrows cannot pierce a dragon's hide.

I can feel all their eyes upon me, and I would do them proud. Breathless silence behind, waiting woods ahead. I square my shoulders and walk beneath the trees.

***

Men's magic is in their seed. That's what my mother told me, when I was a girl. It's what makes them relaxed and steady, good at the patient things in life like planting, growing, and tending. Men's magic flows cool and steady their whole lives. It's the nurturing brook, the calming rain. Of course, women are different.

***

The trees soar, dense and hoary, to the sky. Branches, thick with dark, broad leaves, blot out the sun and cast the forest floor in perpetual twilight. This is nothing like the airy cathedral of the Spring or Summer Woods, where deer graze beneath golden boughs and drink from dancing streams. Nothing like the Autumn Woods either, where fallen pine needles carpet the forest floor in red, and quick-footed ermine haunt the riverbanks.

I know those woods as well as I know my own body, every curve and swell an old, familiar friend. These woods are a stranger. I cannot trust them.

The ground beneath my feet is treacherous, heaved and buckled around giant, worm-like roots and littered with deadfall. Thick vines embrace the monstrous trunks, bedecked with opulent flowers, purple and moist. If I step too close, the blooms contract and billow like puff-balls, letting off a cloud of … something. Spores, maybe. The scent is thick and familiar, but I can't place it.

Deeper and deeper into the woods I walk, my spear loose and ready in my good left hand. The walls and the city are far behind now, out of sight. I have nothing left to prove, no honor to maintain. I could stop if I wanted. Sit on a mossy log in this alien forest and cry for the family and loved ones I left behind. I'm sure others have. I could let myself be scared. There's no shame in fear. I could give up, lie down, turn roots into a cradle for old bones, and wait for the dragons to come. Or I could get angry. The fire is there; I feel it running hot circles round my stomach and behind my ribs. I could beat my chest and rend my hair and scream my rage. Fifty-one years. I wasn't ready to say goodbye!

But I do none of those things. I may be going to feed the dragons, but I don't intend to let them have me without a fight.

***

Women's magic is in our blood. My mother told me

this, too. It makes us strong and fierce and fast, good at the hard and painful things in life like birth, war, and hunting. Our magic is fire and lightning. It burns so hot that when not used for training or growing and feeding children, it must spill over or consume us. That's why women bleed. To let off the extra. Our monthly blood cools us just enough that we can live safely behind the walls with others. Just enough to be sisters, and wives, and mothers.

Until it stops.

***

Hours have passed and still I walk. Step by step, one foot in front of the other. There is no path to follow so I make my own, winding between and around the massive trunks, climbing over roots and stones. I slash aside the vines and their ripe cargo and wish I had a machete instead of a spear.

My feet are tired, and my scars burn. The place on my shoulder where they pulled the arrow out, the old sword-slash on my thigh. My pelvic floor too, because bearing children is its own kind of battle, and I birthed four. There's a hot and heavy feeling down there like I'm carrying around a boulder. Makes me need to piss, but even after I do, it's still uncomfortable. My right knee's the worst; it was never the same after I fell off my horse chasing a fourteen-point stag. Got him too, even after the fall, though it took me a week-and-a-half to get him home. Now there's a dull ache and a sharp stabby feeling every time I move, and I know if I don't get off it and put it up soon it'll be swollen tomorrow.

I laugh at that, a harsh little sound that echoes under the trees. What am I worrying about? There'll be no tomorrow for me. Night is falling in the Winter Woods. There's not much difference, visually. Sunlight, moonlight, starlight: all eaten by the canopy. But there's a difference, all the same. I can hear them creeping through the woods around me. Branches snap, leaves shift. So many of them, circling. Their breath whispers in the still air, their claws scrape like knives on wood and stone. Night is falling in the Winter Woods, and the dragons are closing in.

***

When a woman's monthly blood stops, there's no outlet for her power. It grows inside her. It makes her stronger and hotter: a better warrior, better hunter, better killer. She not safe when that happens. No one's safe.

That's why, when the blood stops for good, the women of my city walk into the Winter Woods to be eaten by the dragons. We defended our city and our families during life, as warriors. In our deaths, we protect them still.

***

It's time. They're all around me. Close. Flitting and flying just out of sight. Creeping towards me. Shadows in shadows, I can't make them out. I feel the breath of wings on my cheeks, the heat of hidden flame on my skin. It's a match for the burning within. I'm feverish and achy, slick with sweat.

I find a giant tree whose tortured roots embrace a swell of stone. I climb and put the tree to my back. There, above the forest floor, protected on three sides, I'll make my last stand. All little girls dream that one day they'll slay dragons. Now it's my turn, and I'll go down fighting.

Will it hurt when they take me? How could it not? Teeth and claws and fire are meant for pain. Will it hurt more than childbirth? Maybe, maybe not. That pain had purpose, but so will this. One to bring new life into the world, one to take a life grown dangerous away. Will I scream? I hope not, but if I do, it's no shame. All I want is to be strong till the end; I think I've managed that.

I draw a slow breath and raise my spear to the slithering, whispering darkness. "Come on then," I whisper. "Come get me." Time to fight dragons. Time to die.

And they're on me. A whirlwind of wings and scales that burn like coals. Flashes of red, and blue, and orange, all fire-hot. Teeth and claws, sharp like knives.

I spin and thrust, only to feel my spear skitter off hard scale. Another blow, another hit, once again turned aside. Am I to be defeated so easily? I scream my rage and strike again, and this time my spear finds a wing. A dragon screams, hot blood gushes down my arms, and I smile. If I am to be a meal, I will be one they remember.

The dragons come at me with renewed frenzy. I'm buffeted, shoved, and spun. A wing hits my head and sends me reeling, and my spear is wrenched from my hands. Talons close on my upper arms and jerk me off the rock. The dragon's skin is hot, and I think it should burn me, but it doesn't. My skin is already burning. I feel like lit tinder, dry and papery and ready to explode into flame. Up, it pulls me. Up, up, up into a seething mass of shadows, and for a moment all I can think is the sky is made of dragons. I'm held arm and leg, and I cannot move.

I close my eyes, clench my teeth, and brace for claws and death.

It doesn't come. Instead, something licks my cheek. Wet and rough and hot, a tongue of flame, and it takes my papery skin with it. I gasp. It's shock, not pain. It should hurt, but it doesn't. Another lick, another swath of dry and crinkled skin gone. The night air is cool against the heat that lies beneath.

Eyes still closed tight, I raise a trembling hand to my face, afraid of what I'll find. Muscle, blood, and bone? My stomach twists, and I hesitate. Or something worse. Something dreamt and then forgotten.

I don't want to touch it, but I do because I promised myself I'd be strong.

There is no gore. My fingers skate over dry, hot scales.

I open my eyes. A dragon hangs before me, holding herself aloft with lazy sweeps of her long, dark wings. Her eyes are filled with fire, but they're familiar all the same. Familiar, beloved, and oh so missed.

"Mother?"

The dragon smiles a sharp and toothy smile, and I'm suddenly aware of my own teeth, hard and long behind dry lips. She nods.

"We don't feed the dragons when our blood stops, daughter." Her voice is a sibilant hiss. It slides between her teeth and into my chest and feeds the flame roaring there. I'm being burned away and remade from the inside out, and it feels like power.

"We become them."

FOUR ACRES AND A SHOVEL
Carman Webb

Nora May saw the truth for the first time on a winter
morning in January. That cold day, Nora got out of
bed, slipped on her robe, and headed for the kitchen,
wondering again why coffee machines aren't kept in
the bedroom. As she waited for the coffee, she ran her
hand up and down the sleeve of the robe she hated. It
was not the first time she had considered her distaste
for something she couldn't bring herself to throw out.
Nora was a woman who liked a routine — and it
didn't make sense to get rid of a perfectly fine robe
whose only offense was to be gray when she would
have preferred to start the morning in a happier color.

     Her first cup of coffee poured into her favorite
mug, she headed back to the bedroom. It was her habit
to slip under the covers with her phone and check in
on the world while she drank the coffee Gideon called
her "get up and go." She glanced at her husband as
she walked into the bedroom, expecting nothing more
than the usual glimpse of his dark hair over the top of
the blankets he kept pulled over his head while he
slept. This morning the blankets were tossed low, as if
Gideon had been about to get out of bed. She noted
the pyjamas she'd given him for Christmas, pleased

again at the way the navy complemented the cream color of their sheets. Her happy thoughts ended there

Where Gideon May should have been, where he had been every single morning since they got married eleven years ago, was a thing Nora couldn't identify. She edged closer. Some strange trick of the light was confusing her. The thing in Gideon's place was hairless, almost translucent, reminding her unpleasantly of a jellyfish washed ashore. It had the same basic shape of a man but seemed smaller than the man she knew. The figure raised a hand to its head and rubbed the top of its bare, wrinkled scalp. That hand was longer and thinner than the hand she held when she went for a walk with her husband in the afternoon sun. The fingers were pointed and knobby in a way that struck her as even more disturbing than the hairless, deflated body before her.

Nora made a noise deep at the back of her throat. She wanted to scream but found her voice was not cooperating. The Gideon-thing sat up and looked at her. Its eyes were pale, and it had no eyelashes. Then it smiled, and she realized its hands were not the most disturbing thing about it. Not even close. Nora understood it was time to be afraid. She'd decided to scream and hurl her coffee in its direction — but she was rooted to the spot. Her body simply would not respond. The thing that didn't look like Gideon, but in some horrifying way reminded her of him, rose from the bed. Before she could react, it was standing in front of her. Gideon/not Gideon reached out to take her coffee cup. The hand that slid across her knuckles was much warmer than she would have guessed. Finally, her body took over, and she passed out.

When Nora opened her eyes, she was staring at her nightstand. She blinked at the alarm clock she never set. It was after nine. She always got up on her own, no need for an alarm, at seven. Always. Nora was a woman who liked a routine.

Behind her, Gideon said, "Good morning."

It sounded like him. And the arm that slid across her and pulled her closer looked like his arm. She grabbed hold of the hand attached to the arm and turned it over in front of her face. The hand wiggled its fingers. She was absurdly relieved to note the swirls of dark hair. Never had she been so relieved to see knuckle hair. She laughed. She felt Gideon rise up on his elbow. She felt him press on her shoulder until she rolled over. She kept her eyes closed for just the space of a breath, but when she opened them the only thing in front of her was Gideon. Gideon with dark hair and brown eyes. Familiar, hairy Gideon. She laughed again.

"I had the craziest dream."

"A funny dream?"

"No," she said quickly. He raised his eyebrows (eyebrows!) at her. "It wasn't funny. Kind of creepy, actually. Guess I'm not feeling very well."

She felt perfectly fine, but nothing less than a slight case of the plague would explain that dream.

Gideon put a hand across her forehead. "No fever," he announced. "Probably just a little PMS. You should've started your period yesterday. Maybe it's coming today."

Nora sighed. She had told him countless times to stop monitoring her cycle so closely. He insisted that it was his duty to keep track of her health. She argued that it was both unnecessary and intrusive. Finally, they had agreed he would at least keep his observations to himself.

"Do you feel like you're about to start?"

She pulled away from him without answering and swung her legs over the side of the bed. She couldn't wait to get outside. Even in January when her garden didn't need her, she stuck to her routine. She stood and glanced over her shoulder. He was lying back against the pillows, scratching softly at his neck.

"I'm not feeling too well myself," he said. "Think I'll sleep just a little longer."

She went to the closet to get her boots. When she came back, he had the blankets pulled over his head. That was when she noticed the coffee mug sitting on the dresser. She stared at it, willing herself to believe there were a million ways her mug could have gotten there. Her hand burned with the memory of hot skin sliding over her knuckles. She shoved her fist in her pocket and left the room, keeping her mind carefully blank. Nora went outside and most certainly did not think about a hairless thing with jellyfish skin and a smile made of nightmares taking a coffee mug from her hand.

During the months it took for her garden to bloom, Nora managed to put the dream out of her mind, at least during the day. Sometimes at night, in that shadowed space between awake and not, a grim certainty took hold that what was beside her in bed was only pretending to be the man she married. On those nights, she put her back to whatever was next to her, refused to look under the covers, and waited for the morning when she could go outside and tend to

47

her garden. Elbow deep in the dirt, the smell of life in her face and sunshine on her neck, she could dismiss what couldn't be true.

Living in the tiny house where she had grown up made it easier to carry on with a routine that did not include contemplating monsters. There were hours to spend in her garden every morning, showers to take in her happy yellow bathroom, work to do in her home office, and movies to watch after dinner. The days were mostly the same as they had been in the two decades since she earned her CPA and converted one room in her house to an office. Back then, Nora Ellison had the vague idea that the third bedroom would be a nursery someday after the right man became her husband. But the years slipped past, and the occasional men were never the right man. Working from home did not lend itself to searching for a husband, particularly when home was on four acres far from neighbors and miles outside of a small North Carolina town that held no interest for anyone not born there.

The third bedroom sat empty behind a closed door until Gideon May showed up on her porch, saying his Jeep had a flat tire. It seemed his cell phone had no reception, and he was looking for a landline. Nora was happy to help the man with dark hair and a cautious smile. After they were married the only thing that was really different about her day were the extra dishes to wash after dinner. Nora mentioned to her new husband that the third bedroom would make a nice nursery, but she was thirty-seven and Gideon needed an office for his graphic design business. That was the end of thinking about babies.

48

Winter conceded to spring, flowers bloomed, and the weeks drifted by without incident. And yet when the nightmare in her husband's clothes stood before her again, she couldn't pretend to be surprised. On that rainy day at the end of April, she stepped out of the shower, thinking nothing more urgent than that it was time to clean the bathroom. It was an easy enough chore. The space was small, barely enough room for two people as Gideon liked to point out, and it took longer to complain about it than it did to clean. Her contented thoughts were interrupted by a sudden, fiery itching at her throat. She was wondering if she had any Benadryl when she saw the reflection in the mirror. A reflection of a pale thing with jellyfish skin and fingers that were too long, scratching its neck. Her mind refused to deal with what stood in front of her. She looked down at her own two hands gripping the towel in front of her naked body. She did not lift her eyes, but she heard the scratching.

"Feels like you're the one with the rash, doesn't it?" The voice was not Gideon's, and yet it was still recognizable as his.

It's Gideon, but not *Gideon all at the same time*, she thought.

"That's a good way to think about it," he said.

How did he know what she was thinking? She looked up despite herself. The thing she had been pretending was a dream grinned at her, and she had never regretted anything as much as she regretted lifting her eyes. The shower was still running, and steam filled the small bathroom. She wished that was enough to blur her vision.

"Did you read my mind?" she asked.

It made a noise that might be mistaken for a laugh by a person who had never known a happy moment. "There are no such things as mind readers," the monster in her bathroom told her. "But I'm very attuned to you. If I'm rested, and I catch you with your natural defenses down, my thoughts can persuade you. Like how I was thinking that this rash is driving me crazy, so you felt it on your neck, too. And just then, how I wanted you to say what you were thinking, and you did it. Didn't you realize you spoke out loud?" Nora turned her face away from the hot blast of its breath and the malicious gleam in its unnatural eyes.

Once, days after they were married, Gideon picked a bowl of wild blueberries and fed them to her in bed while they watched *Titanic*. Giddy with the sweetness of blueberries and new love, she'd imagined all the romantic days ahead. When it turned out Gideon preferred *her* to pick the fruit, she told herself it didn't matter because her husband was a good man. Now the Gideon thing stood in front of her dressed in his clothes, but again she noticed that it was slightly smaller than the man she married. The shirt slid off its shoulder, and it tightened Gideon's favorite belt as she watched. She tried to focus on the sound of the water hitting the happy yellow tile she loved so she wouldn't have to hear the slither of jellyfish skin against the pants she had just washed for her husband yesterday. She shuddered, and the Gideon thing reached around her to turn the water off. She could practically see the shoulder bones moving underneath its thin skin.

"Sit down."

She sat on the side of the bathtub, still clutching the towel in front of her. "What've you done with my husband?"

"I'm your husband. You know that."

She shook her head and then kept shaking it. "No. No. No, you're not Gideon May."

The thing pretending to be Gideon put its hand under her chin until she stopped moving. Its skin was as hot as she remembered. She leaned back until it dropped its hand.

"No need to be shy now, Nora. I've touched a lot more than your face." Her stomach clenched, and she instinctively slapped a hand over her mouth. It smiled that terrible smile again. She dropped her hand to her lap, careful to avoid any sudden moves, and examined the creature in front of her. She wanted very much to decide that this was not Gideon, but the way it tilted its head to the left as it watched her, the way it stood with its hands loose at its side — these things were Gideon.

It couldn't be true. Nora stood, ignoring the towel that fell to her feet. "For the last time, what've you done with my husband? Where is Gideon May?"

"Oh, Nora. I expected more of you. I am what you married. I know your garden is your favorite place in the world. I know you wanted that third bedroom to be a nursery, but you gave up that dream without a fight just to make me happy. You snore, and you're an awful, awful cook. You're allergic to mushrooms. I know you drink a shot of vodka every night before you come to bed and that you like it when I nibble on your neck. I know that you haven't had a period in four months."

She should not be this close. She needed space to manoeuvre. She needed to keep it distracted. "Alright, Gideon. Why do you look like this now?" She sat down again to pick up the towel from the floor. "Why show yourself to me?" When she rose, she moved to the side so she could wrap the towel around herself.

"It takes a lot of energy to put on the Gideon show. It's like a camouflage. A way to keep myself safe. But it's draining to maintain, and you're not giving me what I need any more, as you can tell by this rash that's driving us crazy."

"What do you want?" She did not care what it wanted. She moved closer to the counter. She wasn't sure she had anything deadlier than disposable razors over there, but she was sure she was going to fight.

"I want what all living things want. I want to live."

If Gideon was in front of her, she would say he was pacing. But this was not Gideon. This was something else, and the way it moved reminded her of being a teenager at the roller-skating rink when they turned on the strobe lights.

"So, go live. I'm not stopping you." She tried to look at the bathroom cabinet out of the corner of her eye. Maybe there was something she could throw at it. Her fingernail file and her toothbrush were the only things she could see.

"Nora."

Her brain pulsed against her skull. Her vision blurred. She raised her hands to her head.

"That's me, I'm afraid. Your heart rate is up. Your adrenaline is going. I'm guessing you're planning your escape. That's not going to happen. You're going to calm down." It pulled her hands away from her head and moved them down to her sides. When it smiled, she tasted bile at the back of her throat. "I know it's rude for a man to tell a woman to calm down, but I guess you'll have to forgive me this time."

Somehow, it was behind her even though she had just been looking into those colorless eyes. Its face was right over her shoulder. She heard it scratching its neck. She felt an urge to scratch her own neck, but her arms were so heavy. She told herself to keep calm and look for a way out. Her vision was wavy, but she managed to wiggle her toes just a little. She stayed still, waiting.

"That's better. You know, you should thank me. The others like me get what they need from fear and anger. But that's no way to live, is it?"

"What are you getting from me?"

"Your hormones were putting off a heat that energized me. The closer I got to you, the healthier I was. Our bond was good for both of us. But now things have changed." It sighed, and it was back in front of her before she could react to its words. "Menopause," it added in case she was confused. She wondered if it was still mansplaining if the pompous ass doing the explaining wasn't exactly a man.

"So, go. Leave. Divorce me."

It nodded. "I could do that. I have my next partner picked out. Maura. She's twenty-five. We've been exchanging texts," it told her with an apologetic pat on her arm. "That's a good age. You were so much older than my usual choice, but honestly, I was in a tough spot when we met. I had to take what I could get."

"Sure," she said, raising her left shoulder slightly when it turned to look at itself in the mirror. It glanced back at her, and she froze.

"I know you don't mean that, Nora. I know you would never just let me go. You love me too much." Its laugh was a gruesome noise, like hunted things screaming in the night. Her skin broke out in goosebumps.

"Just kidding. I realize your feelings have probably changed." It shrugged at its reflection. "You could just let me move on with Maura, but I know you won't. You'd be worried about her, wouldn't you?"

"No. I'm not worried about Maura. She's a grown woman. And you aren't going to hurt her." The more it talked, the easier it was for her to move. She ran through a mental inventory of everything in the bathroom — there had to be something heavy to use as a weapon.

"That's true. I've got no reason to hurt her. Not for a very long time."

She could still feel the Gideon thing in her head, trying to keep her in place. She didn't move a muscle. It looked directly at her, and she concentrated on keeping her face blank and her heart steady.

"You can still help me. And anyway, it's not like I can leave a witness. Can't have you telling stories about me. I've learned that lesson. No. It's best we have a clean break."

"A clean break," she repeated. Anything to keep it talking. "What does that mean?"

"I told you there are some like me who take

what they need from fear and anger. It's like a sugar high. But it means you've got to move around a lot, and it's just not the life for me. I prefer the blood bond. I like to find out that a woman's allergic to mushrooms. And that she likes my mouth on her neck." It was right in front of her now. She heard a faint clicking, like maybe it was flicking its tongue against the roof of its mouth. It started to move around her in a circle. Again, she had the disorienting sensation that it moved faster than she could process.

"But right now, a sugar high is just what I need." It stopped in front of her. "In honor of the years we've spent together, I promise you won't suffer. Too much."

Nora bit down hard on the inside of her jaw. The flash of pain cleared her vision immediately. The Gideon thing opened its mouth. Its teeth were improbably long and jagged. Surely, they weren't that long before. It stepped closer and took hold of her shoulders. Its hands were so hot that she winced. In fact, there was so much heat coming off the thing that she broke out in a sudden sweat. *My first hot flash*, she thought.

Those sharp, sharp teeth were getting closer. She dropped her eyes so she didn't have to look at them or think about how wide its mouth had become. Rearing back, she raised an elbow and rammed it with all of her strength into the thing's chest. Gideon/not Gideon stumbled backward. She did not hesitate, did not give it a second to regain its balance. She lunged, hitting it in the chest again. Its arms pinwheeled, but it didn't fall. Her nail file sat on the counter. She grabbed it and held it in front of her with both hands,

55

launching herself at the thing she married. The file sank into its neck, and it stumbled backward and finally went down, smacking its head on the toilet as it fell. The crunch of bone against porcelain echoed in the small room. She seized the curling iron from the counter and wrapped the cord around its neck. It struggled at first, but it was bleeding and dazed.

She was merciless. She pulled the cord tighter, thinking about Gideon May, who never once washed a dinner dish. Gideon who had the habit of drinking directly from the milk container, never asked her how her day was, never said, "Bless you," when she sneezed. There was another dreadful crunching noise under her hands, but she decided not to think about that.

The thing beneath her stopped moving, but she pulled on the cord until she felt her own skin tear. Finally, she stood and looked down at the dead thing on the floor. She unwrapped the towel from around her body and dropped it over the mess. She should be thinking about her next steps, but instead her mind wandered to the movies Gideon liked to watch. He had a fondness for movies where the hero made sarcastic comments while pulverizing bad guys. She nudged the towel with her toe, just to be sure. She had earned the right to a sarcastic comment or two, but really all she wanted to do was get everything cleaned up, just as she had planned when she started her day. She was a woman who liked a routine.

Nora Ellison looked around, at her small yellow bathroom in her tiny house. She could get it all back in order before dark. She made a mental note to find Gideon's phone. Those texts to Maura would come in handy if anyone ever asked about the man who once lived here. She wondered if the thing with skin that made her think of jellyfish would burn. If not, no worries.

She had four acres and a shovel.

NOBODY WARNS YOU
D.A. Jobe

The tree was a massive American beech with a trunk as big around as a cement drainage pipe, and Christ, it had hit with the force of one.

How did Clarke survive this?

Agent Andrea Fernsby high-stepped over downed branches that a week ago would have been eighty feet up in the canopy. In her fifteen years with the park service, she'd watched similar behemoths cut down to clear trails, one section at a time, slabs hitting the earth with a ground-shaking thud. Nobody had felt this one, 1,053 meters up Gray Moth Mountain, except for the five hikers unlucky enough to pitch their tents in the crush zone.

A cooling breeze blew wispy strands of Fernsby's brown hair around her face and rustled the leaves overhead. The beech had taken out a swath of smaller trees, creating snags that made her nervous as hell. One strong gust and more trees could topple over. Trunks rubbed together with an eerie creaking sound. She'd have to pitch her own tent far back from those hazards.

The cicada song was so constant it sounded like water spraying from a showerhead as Fernsby finished her initial sweep, picturing where each of the three tents had been located, by the bright orange Xs spray-painted on the tree trunk.

Had the women felt the impact? She liked to think that even if they had, it wasn't for more than a nanosecond, their human brains so overloaded with pain signals it hadn't registered.

Four had died. The fifth, Meghan Clarke, survived five days pinned under a limb.

Search and rescue had sawed the tree into lighter sections to pull the bodies out — what was *left* of them — along with gear and personal effects. A crew would be up in a day or two to clear the rest of the tree for anything still under it.

Perspiration dotted Fernsby's upper lip and forehead as she waded through a field of broken branches and leaves to a yellow reflective ribbon tied around a tree. It marked where a trail cam had been found, put there by *Press Pause Adventures.* Fernsby felt a flare of anger at the cutesy name.

She shrugged off her heavy pack, rolled her shoulders, then rummaged inside for her own cam, strapping it in the same place. *Let's see what we catch tonight.*

A cloud passed over the sun as she lugged her pack over to a rotting log and sat down against it, adjusting her sidearm holster. She took off a boot and shook it out.

Why the hell am I out here?

Local police had examined the site with search and rescue nine days ago, concluded it was a freak accident. So why had she insisted on hiking up here herself to look around?

Because these women shouldn't have even been here.

The four women's families — *families*! — had hired an unlicensed "wilderness therapy" company to forcibly escort them here for an extreme outdoor experience for menopausal women that promised to help them *embrace the change.*

"Outward Bound for grannies." This from Agent Craig in her office when he'd heard Fernsby was coming up here.

Asshole.

The falling tree might have been an accident, but *Press Pause Adventures* was ultimately responsible. If Fernsby had anything to do with it, nobody involved with that company would be able to prey on another woman again.

She took her tablet out of her pack and tapped a file on the home screen. The first trail cam image popped up. Black and white, low-res. Taken at night, with infrared. It was hard to make out details in the sun's glare, but she'd already viewed the pictures dozens of times. Taken the night before the women arrived in camp, the camera had captured a coyote with a bald spot on its haunch loping past, a flash of reflective eyes.

Bad Penny.

Fernsby's nickname, because the scrawny coyote would show up in the pictures repeatedly over the next five days while Meghan Clarke lay pinned.

SAT 08-09-2018 01:24:20AM

The trail cam needed three seconds to recover

60

between each shot, so there were only two blurry images of the tree mid-fall. In its path: three tents. Four seconds, maybe five. That's all the time the women had. Scrolling rapidly between the pictures, Fernsby could reverse the tree's fall, freeze it so that it hung suspended over the sleeping women. Then, *crash*. A cloud of dust and debris hung in the air.

According to Meghan Clarke's witness statement, the group had been on the trail two days at that point, hiked ten hours up Grey Moth Mountain before making camp.

Fernsby got to her feet with the tablet, went back to the image with the still-intact tents. Tent One: bisected by the thickest part of the trunk. Brooke Banks, white, twenty-seven, field instructor from *Press Pause*, crushed.

Tent Two: hit by a primary limb thick as a person's waist. Helene Parker, Black, fifty-six, broken neck, ruptured organs. Victoria McKay, white, forty-nine, soft tissue damage, fractures.

Tent Three: damaged by secondary branches. Sidney Rees, white, fifty-seven, crushed skull. Meghan Clarke, white, fifty-two, broken legs, bruising.

Fernsby squatted by the orange X where the tree had been cut to extract Banks' body and felt the two-inch deep trench where the force of the tree compacted hard soil.

She snapped a picture, stood, and walked around the beech tree to snap more. Birds flitted overhead.

Helene Parker's sister was pushing to have a memorial service up here. Parker — the only one of the women who'd actually signed up for *Press Pause*'s program. A successful business owner, Parker had admitted to her sister that menopause was kicking her ass. She'd hoped the trip would revitalize her. She'd fully intended to beat her hormone-induced fatigue and anxiety by sheer will.

All four "clients" suffered from mood swings, erratic behavior, depression, anger issues, all brought on by menopause, from what family members told police. Fernsby had zero sympathy for these families (aside from Parker's) regardless of how upset they appeared in front of the cameras: *We thought it would help her. We never would have agreed to it if we had known.*

Searching the ground, Fernsby found and photographed dark, irregular stains in the dirt. Nine days ago — five days after the tree fell — rescuers had arrived to a gruesome scene they described in an incident report, which Fernsby re-read on her tablet now.

Victims' remains show substantial postmortem animal activity.

Evidence of carnivore damage.

SAT 08-09-2018 01:28:36AM

The limb that had ripped through Clarke and Rees' tent, leaving it open to the elements, was as big around as Fernsby's thigh. Rescuers had had to cut it into pieces to get the women out. Clarke said she came to a few minutes after the tree fell, her face entirely covered with leaves. Her movements triggered the trail cam, which also caught a flash of pale skin as she reached for Rees, whose body would have still been warm.

Fernsby clicked over to a transcript of Clarke's videoed police interview: *I reached over to see if she was OK, but she wasn't moving. I remember I felt bad, because I'd been so annoyed with her the day before. Halfway up the mountain she just sat down. Said her pack was too heavy. Brooke threatened to leave it. But the rest of us didn't have enough rations to feed Sidney too. So we took turns carrying her stuff. Her whining the whole time. 'I'm not supposed to be here.' 'There's been a mistake.' I was like, no shit. None of us is here because we want to be. Even Helene, whatever she says.*

SAT 08-09-2018 11:16:02AM

Mid-afternoon on the mountain, Fernsby set up her tent (away from the snags) and collected firewood. It was hot, even under the trees. In the shade of her tent, on her sleeping bag, she flicked through multiple trail cam photos taken in daylight that looked identical. Fernsby had been over these but couldn't discern what had triggered the camera. Probably just Clarke's movements shaking the leaves. She said she'd been in and out of consciousness. The cam's position, and the tree, which took up almost the entire frame, limited the view to just one area.

Bad Penny appeared again. Only feet away from where Clarke was pinned. Muzzle up, sniffing the air. Probably just curious. In the next picture, Clarke appeared to be hurling something at it, a rock or a stick. The animal took off.

Clarke's interview transcript: *After I saw the coyote, I tried to get my knife, but it was in a pocket jammed upside down against the tent floor. The pack was beside me, but I didn't know if it was somehow propping the limb up. I was afraid if I took anything out, more weight would come down on me. I could reach my water. I only let myself have a sip. I knew this was bad.*

Clarke survived the next five days in her sleeping bag, with half a bottle of water, a headlamp, sunscreen, some jerky, three protein bars, and a canister of bear spray.

***

When Fernsby crawled out of her tent a while later, low, misty clouds obscured the treetops. She walked over to where Clarke had been pinned, then laid on the ground on her back, wiggling into the same position Clarke had been in when she was rescued. Broken branches formed a leafy crown around Fernsby's head. She stared up at the cloudy sky through swaying boughs, imagining the limb's weight bearing down on her thighs like a safety bar on a carnival ride. Hundreds of miles of forest stretched around her.

Clarke had presented hypothermia signs at the time of rescue. Her hallucinations seemed to have started on night two from what she stated in her interview. She claimed to have seen something large and stooped, with a leathery sheen, like a beetle's outer shell, moving through the trees. A thing she had called *Coggleclaw*. Gibberish, her husband told police. A silly word their daughters had made up when they were little.

Fernsby fingered the gouges in the hard dirt where Clarke had scratched through the tent vinyl trying to access the pocket with the knife in it. Her fingernails had been torn off when she was found.

A raindrop hit Fernsby's cheek, and she pushed herself up. That's when she saw the paper wedged under a loose piece of bark. Her pulse revved. She grabbed her evidence kit, and — using tweezers — extracted the paper, which had been tightly folded into a thin ribbon. She saw sign of writing but couldn't risk opening it to read. The paper was almost pulp from exposure to the elements. She slid it into a plastic baggie, out of the rain.

SUN 08-10-2018 12:32:19AM

I tried to keep it together by creating a routine. Scheduling meals, singing, counting birds, thinking about what I was going to do when I got free, arching my back, wiggling my toes, digging for the knife. I went through every possible scenario for escape. I tried not to think about dying. I plucked leaves away from my face so I could see out.

I stopped doing that after the second night.

***

Fernsby ate a handful of almonds as she read more of Meghan Clarke's interview transcript, then closed the tablet and laid back on a balled-up sweatshirt. The rain — just a sprinkle — had stopped, but the wind

65

had picked up in the last hour, sending leaves spinning down from the treetops to ping against the tent.

Fernsby had reviewed the trail cam images from Clarke's second night alone; there was nothing to see. Just a raccoon rummaging for food among the women's belongings. Very little movement from Clarke herself. You wouldn't even know she was there, under all those leaves.

As Fernsby's eyes grew heavy, she wondered if she would have managed as well as Clarke had, even with all her experience. Between the sensational headlines (`Secret Adventure Camp for Troubled Women Investigated for Grisly Deaths`), and late-night TV jokes (*How do I sign up my wife?*), Clarke and the other victims were almost being painted as unhappy, angry, hysterical old women who'd had it coming to them.

The cicadas outside Fernsby's tent suddenly went quiet, as if something startled them.

Squirrel.

Maybe a bear.

MON 08-11-2018 2:14:22AM

Darkness crept over the mountain. As the temperature dipped, Fernsby started a fire with damp wood and put her sweatshirt on. The cicadas and birds had fallen silent, the night insects starting up. The crackling fire, the *chirrs* and *clicks*, the pine scent evoked romanticized scenes of camping. Not for Meghan Clarke, who'd spent long, dark nights alone and in pain, no fire to protect her.

Bad Penny had showed up again Clarke's third night, its slinky movements captured by the trail cam. It had sniffed near Clarke's location — so damn close — then sharply turned its head, as if hearing something, before running off. A bright light appeared under Clarke's leaves. Her headlight beam. The ball of light moved erratically in the pictures. What did she hear? Bad Penny? Something else?

The fire popped, and Fernsby jumped. *Jesus*! She exhaled a laugh and slid her hands into the sleeves of her sweatshirt.

Clarke said something in her interview that Fernsby thought about now. *People ask me why I didn't fight. Why I followed Brooke Banks up that mountain. I felt like the worst wife and mother in the world. If the tree hadn't fallen on me, if I'd finished out the program, I think I would have gone home.*

I can never go home now.

***

Fernsby put a pot of water on the fire and scrolled through the next trail cam photos while she waited for it to boil. A couple of hours after Bad Penny's arrival and exit, two bears had shown up at the accident site, disappearing out of view behind the tree. The *carnivores* who'd inflicted damage on the bodies.

She swiped to the next photo, straightened, swiped back. Examined the edge of the frame. Two pinpoint lights suggestive of eyes. In the trees. Another bear? No, the eyes, if that's what they were, were too high off the ground.

The Coggleclaw.

The hair on the back of Fernsby's neck lifted. *It's just a trick of the light.*

She scrutinized until her nose almost touched the screen, but the more she tried to make the shadow take shape, the more it looked like nothing.

MON 08-11-2018 6:56:39AM

Fernsby ate her soup before looking at the trail cam images taken on Clarke's third sunrise on the mountain, when a bird had triggered the cam. Victoria McKay's severed arm was hard to see in black and white, poking out of the bushes at the edge of the frame, indistinguishable among the scattered branches. Her wedding ring was still on her finger.

Right before McKay's husband had sent her off to *get herself sorted out* (his words), the lady had apparently taken the keys to his antique Corvette and driven it 90 MPH down gravel roads, rock-blasting the paint off the sides. Fernsby snorted a laugh when she'd heard that.

In her interview, Clarke had said that during some kind of menopause-consciousness-raising session led by Banks — *ugh* — McKay had described feeling like she was a residual haunting in her own home, moving through the motions of her life with no interaction from her family. Of all the *Press Pause* clients, McKay seemed to have really gotten into the experience. *Vicky was so proud of herself after finishing that ten-hour hike*, Clarke remembered. *She said she felt strong.*

Clarke had not known whose blood-spattered arm it was she saw that third morning, but she dug frantically for her knife that day.

A terrible thought came to Fernsby then as she stared at McKay's arm in the picture, bright white bones visible in the stump.

What if McKay was still alive when the bears ate her?

MON 08-11-2018 02:26:11PM

Light rain fell on Fernsby's fire, hissing and popping in the embers. After banking the fire, she crawled into her tent and checked the radar. Thunderstorm coming. She flicked on a lantern, zipped into her sleeping bag.

If any of the accidents Fernsby had investigated, where the victim survived, had anything in common, it was the Fluke Effect: a fall broken by a soft bed of undergrowth that just happened to be there. A chance ledge in a slot canyon as a flash flood crashes through.

The sequence of events leading to Clarke's rescue was almost elegant in design, or cosmically lucky, depending on how you looked at it.

The pesky coyote, Bad Penny, was Clarke's Fluke Effect.

Fernsby viewed the trail cam images now: Bad Penny dragging Brooke Banks' daypack a few feet from where Clarke was concealed by leaves. Suddenly darting off, chasing after the piece of jerky Clarke had thrown. Over three agonizing hours, Clarke managing to snag the pack with a broken branch and pulling it to herself.

Inside, she had found Banks' personal locator beacon device and pushed the SOS button.

That's when I was the most scared, Clarke had said in her interview. *I didn't know if the beacon worked. I forced myself not to hope. Another night came and I didn't sleep. I held that bear spray tight. I heard noises. Footsteps. Bones ... cracking. I heard the Coggleclaw breathing. I* smelled *it. It smelled like blood.*

The trail cam images taken around that time show the bears had returned, settling down not far from Clarke, feeding on Rees, lifting their heads as if sniffing Clarke but staying back.

TUES 08-12-2018 07:52:46AM

The next cam image was triggered by a blackbird the next morning, pecking at something on the ground.

The carnage was sickening, even in black and white.

Fernsby checked if her sidearm was loaded.

TUES 08-12-2018 05:29:01PM

The locator beacon had worked. Clarke's rescue was captured in hundreds of images before the trail cam was taken down. After scrolling to the last picture, Fernsby cut off the tablet and lantern, plunging the tent into darkness.

***

She blinked awake. Rain pounded the tent. She checked her watch: 2:16 A.M. As she was about to drift off again, she heard a crunching noise in the

70

woods. Footsteps. Moving almost timidly.

Fernsby relaxed. *Just a deer.*

But as she lay there with her eyes closed, Clarke's words wormed their way into her brain: *I heard the Coggleclaw breathing. I* smelled *it.*

It smelled like blood.

Fernsby's eyes snapped open. Another footstep. Right behind the tent.

Chill. It's just an animal.

It crept around the side of her shelter.

Heart racing now, Fernsby slipped from the sleeping bag as quietly as she could, reached for her gun. Crept to the tent opening, gripped the zipper pull. She took a deep, silent breath. Then yanked the zipper down and scrambled outside in one motion with her gun raised.

Something big and dark blundered by her, crashed into the underbrush and dissolved into the night.

Something that had a sheen to its body.

Something that smelled like blood.

WED 08-22-2018 12:29:34AM

Fernsby lost whatever it was in the forest. But the trail cam caught it as it fled. Victoria McKay, in a dark rain poncho with a backpack underneath.

Back in the office, Fernsby pored over the trail cam images and forensic analysis. The severed arm they'd *thought* was McKay's was actually Rees'. McKay had evidently found the limb, removed Rees' wedding ring, and placed her own on the dead woman's finger, presumably to make it seem like she'd died in the accident. And she'd counted on the fact that the authorities would dismiss the deaths of five women — four of them fifty-plus — as just a tragic accident. Which they had, until Fernsby took up the case.

Fernsby would probably never be able to prove it, but she could picture McKay lurking around the site, hoping the animals would eat and scatter the remains. Waiting, perhaps, for Clarke to die. Not having the stomach to kill her herself.

Victoria McKay had wanted to disappear. And she had.

No trace of Victoria McKay was ever found.

***

Letter submitted as evidence in the case against Archie Clarke, accused of false imprisonment by ex-wife, Meghan Clarke.

Meg, The girls and I talked, and we thought this program would help you. Please don't fight. We'll be here when you get back.

IN BLOOM
Dr. Bunny McFaddden

Mark slid the straw in and out of his cup, enjoying the way it made his boss twitch. He knew she wasn't going to stop her presentation on the jellyfish blooms just to tell him to cut it out — especially because his dad was listening in on the telecom.

He slid it again, drawing out the squeak so that it sounded like a mouse in a kill trap. This meeting was a joke. He didn't even want to work in the biology department, but they needed an intern and he needed something for his resume. All he wanted to do was pull on his wetsuit and get out there in the sun before White Boy Summer was over. Instead he was stuck in this office watching Jenny sweat in front of her webcam.

"Who the fuck cares about jellyfish blooms," he wanted to ask her.

Instead, the moment she thanked the postdocs and hung up, he said, "Wow, Jenny. You're sweating a lot." He took the napkin from under his cup and slid it to her, enjoying the way she squinted at the plastic straw. "Hot flash?"

"You know those are bad for the turtles, Mark," she said, dabbing at her forehead. "And I've

73

asked you to call me Dr. White."

"What's the big deal? It's not like anybody else is in the office," Mark replied, leaning forward to suck down the Sprite.

Jenny folded the used napkin deliberately. He could tell she was about to launch into another of her lectures.

But instead, she closed her laptop and walked out of the conference room toward her office. That was weird. Mark shrugged and crumpled his fast-food bag into a balloon. Through the open door, he saw her. He smacked the bag so that it popped, sending a cloud that smelled of grease and salt up into his face and a clap that echoed down the corridor. Dr. White jumped in her skin. A little fear was good for her. It kept her on her toes. Livened up the place. He smirked with satisfaction.

***

The time from lunch until Mark was allowed to leave at 4:00 was the worst part of his day. Sure, there were files he could digitize, stacks of field notes that smelled of salt and proved Dr. White actually did exist out of the office and occasionally even went to the beach. But the hum of the scanner put him in a catatonic state, one that even the schnapps he snuck into his lunch Sprite wouldn't fix, and he wanted to be on his A-game this evening. There was going to be a big beach bash to celebrate that the Oceanic Studies Center got some grant or something. Maybe he'd finally see Jenny in a swimsuit. She'd brought a tote bag to the office today.

Like most times when he was bored, Mark went to the office bathroom. He left the door unlocked for the extra sense of thrill. One day, she'd walk in. He fell into a familiar fantasy about his boss' body in a bikini, her curly brown hair falling in waves that he could almost feel his hands grasping. When he was done, he left the wadded toilet paper on the edge of the porcelain sink.

***

At 3:59, Mark walked into Jenny's office, jingling his keys. She sat at the desk, glasses reflecting her screen, and barely noticed.

"You want a ride in my Jeep?" he said, reaching down to pick up her tote bag.

She was next to him in a flash. She yanked the bag out of his hand. "Don't touch things that don't belong to you."

But he'd already seen what was in the bag. A skimpy swimsuit. For a moment, he could practically picture her in it. He stared at her tight body hiding from him under the silk shirt. But as he leered, he saw sweat stains on her blouse. Gross.

***

The waves were dark by the time he convinced Jenny to swim with him. Plying her with his schnapps had helped. And he reminded her that the cool ocean water might feel nice. It would be good for her.

"After all," Mark cajoled, "I know you're going through the change. My mom went through it last summer. I can tell."

They were up to their thighs now. Something briefly swished against his leg.

"You're right," Dr. White said. "I feel so free!" Her swimsuit was nothing like he expected. No, it was better. It was almost translucent in the water, a series of strings and loops and white fabric that tauntingly covered her body. The sun had set, but she seemed to almost glow.

"Bioluminescent," he muttered, slurring the word as he stared at her gelatinous tits. The way they seemed to float and bob each time a wave lapped against her baffled him.

"Oh, not bioluminescent, Mark, that's not how this works," his boss said. "You really haven't learned anything from your internship, have you?"

He laughed nervously and reached out to touch her arm. The ocean felt delightfully cold against his flesh. Jenny smiled at him, a wave rolling her just out of reach.

"What's the matter, Mark?" she said, swaying as the waves gently tugged at her thighs. "Do you want to go deeper?"

"Why is the water so cold all of a sudden?" he asked. "Wait, wait, I think we should get out now, Jenny."

"I told you to call me Dr. White," she said, coming closer, almost stalking him as he struggled toward the shore.

"I'm serious, Jenny," he said. "Are you having a hot flash or something? You don't feel that?" The cold spot swirled violently around him, the waves foaming as if they were boiling. Mark's legs were

76

sluggish, frozen. How could they be moving this slowly? He kicked, but his skin stung. The burning sensation spread, rising up into the cuffs of his swim trunks.

"Feel what?" Jenny laughed. Her voluminous hair looked almost like it was floating in the moonlight.

The sensation was starting to go painful. The water wasn't just cold. He looked down. Hundreds of tiny jellyfish cloistered around him. They were in a bloom.

He desperately turned away from her — every man for himself, like his father said — but a current seemed to suck at his feet, holding him in place.

"Where are you going, Mark? The bloom's just starting." She laughed again as he struggled. "I thought you said you knew about my change."

The translucent bikini glowed, its strings defying gravity as they squirmed. He blinked, unable to process what he was seeing. Before his eyes, she was morphing. The lithe arms he'd pictured pinning against the office wall had gone from smooth and tan to bubbling with spiny tentacles. Her chest writhed, melding with the bikini top. Floating bodies of jellyfish bumped into his now-numb body, and he felt himself slipping into unconsciousness. Another sting jolted him.

"Oh no, you don't, big boy," she said, her voice like a siren. "You've been staring at me all summer. Now it's time to really see me."

Her hands pulled on his shoulders, keeping him just above the water. Her fingers stuck to him like suckers, glued to his back, wrapping around his arms, everywhere at once, bruising his flesh.

"It's funny," she said. "You think being spineless makes us weak." She tugged him closer. He kicked his legs in a final fit of panic.

"But you don't need a spine here."

TRANSCENDING
Julie Ann Rees

I felt it arrive, squatting on the periphery waiting to pounce, catch me unawares, but I knew it was coming. My hair had begun to fall out; great tendrils trailed black and tangled in my hairbrush and blocked the sink. I changed shampoo, opting for natural vegan formulas, but it did no good. I decided to stop dyeing my hair, in case the dye was causing the hair loss. Now a few inches of coarse grey accentuates the bare scalp of my ever-expanding middle parting, my dark hair hanging floss-like in comparison.

Having been a thin person my entire life, I didn't expect the blubber that grew and hung from my middle. A pouch formed and expanded; now I sit bloated, spider-like, fretting and knitting with my scrawny arms. I knit to keep busy whereas I used to be active, but now my joints hurt and I get tired so quickly. I catch a glimpse of myself in the reflection of the silent TV, hunched and hag-like. Shuddering, I place the knitting down and decide to shower, put some makeup on, tidy myself up.

Almost overnight my skin has sagged. I've always had laughter lines, but now they're more like grinning grooves and I have jowls. My features have collapsed, and the makeup I've always worn transforms me into a pantomime dame, both crass and cheap, a parody of my former self — the self I see inside my head, the self I've always recognised as me. The image that scowls back is not me, can't be me. I won't let it in. I return to my knitting, defeated.

I remember being pregnant with my daughter and on holiday in France. An old woman caught my eye in the market square of a provincial village. Crone-like, she sat sniggering and grinning, pointing to my small bump that was hardly showing as I was only about four months gone. I tried to avoid her gaze but found myself enclosed in a crush of people and pushed towards her table and wares. She spoke to me; my French was not great, so I feigned disinterest, but she grabbed my arm. Sun-browned fingers, old bone and sinew, curled gently but firmly, and her voice cackled *your baby will drink your beauty*.

I stepped back, shocked, but she turned her attention to selling some pickled preservative to a German man at my side, allowing me to scurry away. I've thought of what she said before but never felt it so much as now. I have been a young girl, pretty and carefree, and a mother, both vain and haughty, morphing into a different kind of beauty; an older, confident beauty but still insecure. Now that mask is slipping, sliding away to reveal the truth, my truth, my transcendence into the final stage — the darker phase. The crone.

My daughter is a beautiful young woman, the embodiment of me at her age, but more confident with a sassy edge. She has moved away to live, a bright star in a darkening universe, while I have no energy for the dreams I hoped to fulfil. Dreams I believed I'd get back to one day in the future before I got too old. My cat Kafka curls on my lap stretching; a claw catches at my knitting, pulling a thread, destroying the pattern.

I watch the thread, the disruption, and quickly try to repair the damage. I unpick and start that row again, conscious of the unfurling wool, and feel my mind unfurling. I have forgotten what I was doing. *Mind fog* the doctor called it, and it comes with the menopause as well as all the other symptoms I am experiencing. I couldn't help finding the young GP attractive, and the knowledge that he probably has a young wife or girlfriend at home sickened me. I was once an attractive, sought-after young girl. Doesn't he realise this, with his looks of pity and condescending smile as he advises HRT? Can't he see what I once was? Can't he see through what I am becoming?

I begin to sweat. It stinks, sour and sickly, clashing with my perfume; even though expensive, it smells cheap and false. Nausea floods me, and I worry I will vomit. Dizzily, I get to my feet and remove my cardigan. I need air, so let myself into the garden. The fresh air cools my skin to goose flesh. A breeze pushes my stench around me so I walk in a cloud of unseen odour, a constant reminder of my body's altering presence.

There is an old cherry tree at the bottom of the garden. The blossom is nearly past — it never lasts long enough. No sooner does it burst forth in beauty than a storm passes and ravages the delicate bouquets. The pink glory damp and browning with decay decorates the floor with a carpet of impermanence. I could sense it strongly. The thing that haunts me, squatting on spindly haunches, watching; blossom stuck to its face with hair hanging in ratty tendrils.

I turn away, shun the feeling, suddenly cold, and hurry indoors; my knees click from the movement, reminding me of my condition. To call it a condition is wrong. It is a process all women go through, like puberty. I hadn't expected to feel so run down is all, I hadn't thought how losing my looks my body my youth my ability to reproduce to procreate...how losing this would leave me so vulnerable. I don't want it to happen; I don't want it to consume me.

Making a cuppa, I watch the thing watching me; it doesn't move, just stares. More blossoms descend to float around it before succumbing to the damp earth that claims all. I bite hard into a bar of chocolate, one of my only pleasures, and my bridge tooth comes loose. I curse my gluttony and quickly spit the bridge out. Regarding myself in the mirror, I smile. The gap shows as my reflection grimaces back. The thing in the garden cackles.

My daughter phoned to say she'd be coming to visit soon; her husband was busy working, and she had some news but wouldn't say over the phone. I'd already guessed she was going to tell me she was pregnant. There was a change to her voice; a motherly tone had overridden the carefree flippancy of her usual conversations. Tears brimmed in my eyes, and I pretended I had no idea and was looking forward to seeing her because it had been too long. Thank God I'd already taken up knitting.

I felt better going to bed that night as talking to my daughter had cheered me. I'd opened a bottle of red wine and maybe drunk a little too much, but I'd gone off like a light.

The dream that descended left me floundering. My work colleagues were cross because I'd been off work too long, so the boss came to get me. I struggled as he dragged me through darkness into a restaurant where a domed wood-burning stove glowed red. He folded me up like a ventriloquist dummy and pushed me into the flames. People were laughing, and a chef with a hat and twirling moustache closed the oven door.

I woke screaming. The sheets were drenched in sweat, and my head throbbed feverishly. Kafka cat leapt from my bed and darted out of the door. I heard the cat flap release him into the night. I lay panting as, slowly, my body cooled to shiver against the now cold, wet bedding. I got up, changed my nightshirt, and stripped the bed. I put on a clean fitted sheet but couldn't be bothered to put on a clean duvet cover, so pulled it over me coverless. I lay there and listened for the thing in the garden. It had entered the house. I could hear it shuffling about downstairs and rummaging through my stuff.

That morning I had a text from Jim asking if I wanted to meet up later. Jim was a divorced man in his late fifties with two grown up kids. We had been seeing each other for a few years. All had been fine until the last few months when I didn't seem to have any energy, and as for my libido, well, it was nonexistent. Jim didn't get it, as we had been like teenagers before, but recently sex had become painful and I kept getting thrush from various lubes and sex toys in a bid to reawaken things. I hesitated to reply but decided to invite him over; he said he'd take me out for dinner so I didn't have to cook.

Whilst making a coffee I noticed rotten cherry blossom squashed across the floor of the kitchen and living room. I remembered the thing had been in the house last night. It had pulled out old photo albums and left them strewn across the settee, pictures of me as a young woman, then as a mother, laughed at me. A plate and bowl were in the sink, so it had eaten. I sniffed the bowl and recognised the sickly-sweet scent of vanilla ice cream. I sat down on the kitchen stool and noticed my slippers had blossom stuck to the pink fluff. My eyes went to the cherry tree and the thing beneath it, crouching amongst the decaying flowers, waiting.

I spent ages deciding what to wear that evening for my date with Jim. All of my clothes had ceased to fit overnight; my figure-hugging dresses revealed hip fat and a bulbous belly. In exasperation, I pulled on an oversized blouse and leggings, ditching the idea of cinching the waist with a belt. As I considered how to apply makeup without appearing to have applied any, I noticed my gap tooth. How could I have forgotten? I couldn't go out like this, and if I wedged the bridge back in I wouldn't be able to eat without risking choking on it. I called Jim to cancel.

Jim, bless him, insisted that he didn't mind my gap tooth, but he didn't understand that I was the one who minded. Just because he liked me didn't mean I liked me. He suggested instead a takeaway of my choice, and he'd bring some wine. All I had to do was open the door when he arrived, and I could even wear my pyjamas if I wanted. I reluctantly agreed and chose Indian because I knew that was his favourite. I knew all he really wanted was sex. It was amazing the lengths men went to get it.

I didn't wear my pyjamas, leaving my blouse and leggings on in a bid to appear normal. He arrived on time as usual, amidst a cloud of spice and fried odours emanating from the carrier bag he held. He'd brought a couple of cold beers and a very good bottle of wine. He smiled, and I realised how lucky I was. He was an attractive man, even more so with his grey hair and he still kept his figure trim. Immediately I felt inferior and frumpish. What the hell was he doing here with a miserable fat, ugly, old cow like me? He entered, and I slammed the door on the cackling I knew would be coming from the cherry tree.

The evening began well, and I even felt my old libido return. One thing led to another, and we ended up in bed. We were both familiar with each other, but I was not familiar with what had happened to my body. It was not pleasurable, and I know Jim felt the change in me. It hurt when he touched me, and I was so dry I could feel my vaginal wall tearing even with the lube that just irritated. Thankfully the wine had dulled my senses, and I turned away from him when he'd finished and descended into a drunken sleep.

I woke to voices arguing. Jim wasn't in bed. I could hear his tones echo up the stairs. A voice not unlike my own but more frantic and screechy was replying, getting louder. Jim was trying to placate them, and a scuffle ensued. I hid, willing myself to become invisible as Jim entered the bedroom. He grabbed his clothes and went back downstairs. More scuffling was followed by a scream. Then I heard Jim say clearly, "You're mad. I've tried and tried but you need professional help." The other voice cackled, and I heard something metallic drop to the floor. The front door opened and slammed as something smashed against it from the inside.

I looked out of the window as Jim hurried down the garden path, struggling to get into his coat. I picked up the kitchen knife where it had fallen and cleaned up the smashed vase that had been hurled against the front door. There was cherry blossom stuck in the carpet and all over my slippers again. Long strands of greying hair were tangled in my fingers, and my scalp hurt where I had been tearing at it. I heard the cat flap, and Kafka entered. He brushed against my legs purring, and I began to cry.

I stopped taking the anti-depressants the doctor gave me and agreed to go on HRT. My daughter was coming to visit, and I wanted everything to be in order — including my brain. I'd been knitting booties in pale green and baby blankets. I'd spoken to her again, and she'd practically confirmed my guess. I was going to be a grandmother. I looked at my reflection and tried to comb my hair over the bald patches that had formed since the night Jim had visited. I'd had one text from him: he hoped I was okay, and we'd better not see each other again, or at least until I got help.

The night before my daughter arrived, I went to bed early. I felt positive, more than I had for some time, although I was a little apprehensive about what she would make of my appearance. I'd still not had my bridge tooth replaced; it took forever to get a dentist appointment these days. Again dreams flooded my mind, and I felt hot, burning hot. The sweat oozed out of my pores, the stench cloying and thick like fat from a roasting pig.

I opened my eyes to the smouldering interior of the domed nightmare oven. Scarlet skin blistered and tingled as I scratched and scrambled, twisting onto my stomach to push at the door. My hands burned, nails breaking like tinder, my hair a halo of fire as the heat roared, and scorching flames licked the soles of my feet, the pain burning up my calves. Screaming, I pounded and woke, scratching at my skin until red and inflamed it bled into the damp sweaty sheets.

Once again I changed the bedding. I was awake now and knew sleep would not return before dawn. Unable to decide if I was hot or cold, I left the duvet on the floor and simply lay upon the cool sheet. I could hear a noise in the hallway. A strange voice humming a tune and footsteps ascending the stairs; slowly they reached my bedroom door. Panicking, I tried to move but found I couldn't. Corded muscles constricted my throat as I struggled to grunt into movement, my breathing getting faster until erratic gasps leapt from my chest.

I felt the thing enter the bedroom. The same screechy, cackling voice that had screamed at Jim now muttered and cooed. Bony hands prodded my stomach, and the voice giggled, dry and rasping. I felt it circle the bed, watching me. Cherry blossom rotten and decayed dropped onto my nightshirt as it clambered over my body. The sour stench of sweat lingered as it passed before squatting by my feet. I looked into a face of wrinkled bark haloed by grey hair wisped sparsely over mottled skin, stretched tight over a skull erect upon a sinewy neck.

I tried to kick it away, tried to get up and run, imagined myself doing this and putting on the light, dispersing the nightmare, but every time I thought I'd woken I found myself back on the bed laid out like a feast. The heat returned, and I could feel myself burning up.

I was back in the restaurant of my dream, displayed on a serving tray, still hot from the oven. The thing sat at the table waiting as silent hands and feet wheeled me closer. I passed other tables where my work mates grinned and raised glasses to me, and there was Jim with a younger woman that looked like I used to.

My feet tingled. The cooked skin blistered and flaked. The thing's nostrils flared and tasted my smell before looking to the chef with the twirling moustache and, smiling, thanked him. The others in the restaurant had stopped their chatter and watched as the thing picked up a serviette and draped it over its lap. It raised a glass of pink blossom to the onlookers, and I heard Jim's voice shout cheers before laughing, and the chatter resumed. The chef twirled his moustache with a flourish and returned to the kitchen.

A tongue shrivelled out from a lipless mouth and slowly licked the dripping fat from the soles of my feet that twitched in reply. It smiled with a gap-toothed grin and opened its mouth, ingesting my toes one by one until my feet too slipped inside the slavering maw. I watched helplessly as the neck contracted to swallow my limbs like a python, the nose stretched wide, the jaw dislocated to receive my body. I swivelled my head towards Jim in a plea for help, but he was engrossed in conversation with the faceless beauty, her back turned firmly against me.

A scream ripped silently through my mind as I watched it slide upwards, devouring my lower self. Eyes like cherry stones widened in mock alarm as its mouth stretched wider to gorge on my stomach. Pointed elbows straddled either side as it clawed forwards with bulging throat to devour my torso and merge with my heart. The jaws closed into a pursed kiss to swallow before clamping over my neck. I tried to struggle to stop the inevitable as wet lips sucked at my chin.

Closing my eyes, I succumbed, gave myself over to the thing as it swallowed the self I would no longer be. The other people had finished their meals, including Jim; they began to leave the restaurant as birdsong dispersed the scene. I felt my breath exit my body in one great sigh before my head transcended and released into a crushing darkness. I lay there, sweat clammy on an old body, wondering what my daughter would think when she arrived to find this hag-like being that had consumed her mother.

INFERNO
Victory Witherkeigh

The cold, wet puddle underneath me is sopping enough that droplets of water have collected between my thighs. I don't even have to open my eyes to know that my bedspread is soaked again. Goosebumps and the slick sheen of sweat pooled at the base of my neck & low back have told me that the night sweats have won once more.

A blaring red light glows through the room as my hand paws across the nightstand, feeling for my glasses. It's gotten to where this routine has numbed me beyond exhaustion. I don't have to turn the lights on to stumble out of my thin — and I mean threadbare — single sheet to pull off the drenched set.

Just give it some time, they said. Your body is still adjusting.

They warned me early in childhood that the women in my family bear a curse. For various periods, my female cousins and I would be sequestered, informed we could not form the bonds with one another often seen with the other island families. No one could tell us when the curse began, only that it had been caused by one of the tribal wars. One of our female ancestors was in the wrong place after the battle, unable to escape with her people. Instead of simply killing her, the chief made her an example, violating her with his troops as a prize.

"It was said that she lay in her own blood for days afterward," my grandma would say. "Silent in such rage as she had cut out her own tongue from her teeth biting down, as though willing herself to deny those monsters her screams, if she could not deny them anything else..."

My large, dark brown eyes widened as she told this story, even as I grew older, and I always asked the same thing every time: "Then what happened, Grandma?"

Her soft, wrinkled face would look at me wistfully, as though even in bearing the curse, we should be proud of this faceless ancestor.

"It took her a few weeks to heal up, but she knew her body well enough to know that they planted a child from that vengeful act. Her nausea rose with the sun and the scent of pineapple and fermenting fish hitting her nose. The humidity made each moment dizzy, as food and water came only three times a day. She knew she'd rather die than bring about any spawn from the monsters who had defiled her..."

I still shiver when I remember my grandmother's face, pale but stern, as she explained further.

"Using what strength she had left, she'd swiped a small blade from one guard during a shift change. Then, under the darkest day, with a full eclipse blacking out the sky, she used this stunted shaft to slice into the flesh of her belly, praying to Sitan as the god of Death to help avenge her people, to accept her sacrifice for the power to destroy her enemies.

"We don't know how long she lay bleeding on the ground," my grandmother would whisper, entranced, her dark chocolate eyes staring out into nothing. "All I know is what my Lola told me, that the ground produced vines but not of any kind of greenery. No, these vines, curling and growing before her were made of hellfire, sizzling and smoking as their tendrils wound and sprouted in various directions.

Germinations of flaming leaves birthed black peppers, glowing with the ashen flame of newly exploded lava as the volcano erupts. The dark god had answered her request, and somehow our ancestor knew she needed to eat the vile, smoking bud of the dead to cement their bargain."

For years as a child, I tried with my cousins to shrug off this story as another old wives' tale from the ancient world where our family came from. I am a first generation American, after all.

What good did the tales of the gods of my ancestors do for me in Los Angeles, California?

I shrugged off my older cousins' disappearances to them growing up, entering high school or college — wanting to make their own way into the world. If I could see my childhood self now, I'd probably slap her for her arrogance.

The curse began with the onset of my period at ten. I was the first in my grade to get it, but I guarantee I was the only one who also received nightmares of what my ancestor became. In eating that hellfire pepper, all she once was as a warrior woman was forgotten. The islands would henceforth only know her as Mantiyanak, or *the Returned*. She became the first vengeance spirit to serve the dark god. The fiery pepper returned her physical strength, gave her a tantalizing tongue, and left her body only with the telltale scar where she carved into her belly. As I entered what society deemed womanhood, I saw her legacy, night after night, in my dreams.

She would not allow the sins of those men to go on unpunished. I could see her beauty, cold and sharp against the moonlight, luring men away from their posts, their families, tempting them with the same sexuality they took from her. Then, at their most vulnerable, her mouth, tongue, and hands became a red, hot hellfire of destruction, burning their mouths and their genitals until they bled out into the night.

The joy in her vengeance meant that her descendants, like me, couldn't be trusted with any man alone. The family tried to let her lineage die out many times, but it seemed she or the god of Death weren't done with their vengeance. I don't know how they continued on with the magic, as those arts are long gone with the old teachings of our culture and language. The colonization of the islands destroyed much of what carried our women through. But with the birth of science and test tubes, children sprang forth again.

I didn't want this kind of fiery hellscape of loneliness for any daughter of mine. Once I discovered the truth of the curse, I swore that I would stop this madness, this destruction. I wouldn't allow my child a lifetime of *no*'s to school dances, boyfriends, or even girlfriends. When I graduated from college, got my first job, I signed up for a hysterectomy. I thought I was brilliant, cutting out the curse from my life.

I was wrong.

Now well into my early thirties, the fire and vengeance that once froze me in place from dating or sex or physical contact eat at my body night after night. I thought that cutting out my uterus would eliminate my bloodlust and drive to kill the surrounding men in my life. Instead, I scour the earth for ways to speed along the destruction of my ovaries left behind. They never told me the curse is tied to the very seeds that bring life to us. Since the hysterectomy, the lust to kill for me is no longer bound to just a particular time of the month. It would be just my luck that I only cemented it further in trying to escape my fate. The night sweats seem to be part of my punishment for trying to bypass the family legacy — my blood now boiling from the unleashed hellfire in my veins.

Just give it some time, they said ... Your body is still adjusting ... Once your ovaries die off and menopause is complete ... It'll stop right?

I finally get to my laundry room, dumping the damp sheets into the washer to start the next cycle. Scents of lavender and jasmine mix in the air with the sound of the click in the washing machine's door as I hit the start button. Opening the dryer, I pull out the crisp beige linens along with a USC sweatshirt, inhaling the smell of cedarwood and jasmine.

My ancestors cackle with laughter and madness behind me. Kill after kill, generation after generation, it's all I can hear as my tongue reaches

forward to lick along a bloodstain on the sweatshirt
that didn't come out in the wash.

     It's the taste I have every morning after a meal
like that one—youthful coppery blood and ash.

FLEDGLINGS/CRONES

B.J. Thrower and Karen Thrower

Mandy hissed at the bound man, "*Worm*! Your wife complained to us, scoundrel!"

Mandy's twin, Candy, laid her hands over his eyes, chanting black magic spell words. He screamed as they both felt the tickle on Candy's palms — of the worms squirming out of his sockets.

"Mandy? Candy!" The six-year-olds saw Mama in the doorway of their shared bedroom, thick, curly black hair bound up in a scarf and her apron covered in flour with one of the servant girls peeking over her shoulder. Worst of all, Mama caught them with a toy that wasn't theirs.

They knew she loved them, but she also wondered about their magical inheritance, and how strong it was becoming. Making no sense to the children, Mama would sigh in doubt and murmur about blood and moons, "I suppose it depends on when their blood moons start, ay? If the courses are spotty or heavy, or last too long, or if the girls have cramps."

Instead, this time Mama merely reminded them: "Please don't break Brother Georgie's doll, hear?"

Nodding, the girls re-focused, concentrating on the carved wooden soldier's face. His features included a vague face and beard no more than black dots, but his uniform was quite nice, precisely painted on the male form in bright red with white trim.

Candy said, "He's not bloody enough."

Mandy smiled. "Get the watercolors, the red especially."

***

Misty/Mandy surveyed her twin sister through the intermittent flames. Night bugs whirred around them, attracted by the campfire in the thickets behind the village, in a secret clearing. At age fifteen, Misty/Mandy was jealous of her sister; it wound through her veins like a snake.

Misty/Mandy figured she was the smartest of the pair of them. They weren't even identical with distinctive faces; Misty/Mandy's plumper, with what she considered a crooked nose, slightly bucked teeth, and plain brown hair. Crimson/Candy was slender, with Mama's abundant black, gorgeous hair, and a pixie's upturned nose. *Willowy,* Misty/Mandy thought in pure resentment.

Adding insult to injury, Crimson/Candy had started her blood moons two damned years ago, while Misty/Mandy hadn't passed a drop o' blood yet! It galled her, even if Crimson/Candy suffered cramps and bloating.

When will it be my time! she wailed to her mother, mindful that on a faraway day the menopause curse would smite them both and end their powers.

But Mama could tell her only: *Soon, my love. Soon.*

Kept within the family, no one else ever knew their double names, a sign of their transition from children to grown women, and a rite of passage for witches. As the village church bells now rang in the distance, the young ladies were busy elsewhere in these wet, springtime woods, with a strange boy and an outdoor fire.

A teenager the same as them, they had coaxed him into the fragrant forest with promises of a jug, and perhaps, kisses. Pretty black skirt lined with red silk along the bottom hem, planted around her on the ground like scattered roses, Crimson/Candy had already used the knife on his bare arms, tracing hex symbols in his flesh as he writhed, tied to stakes with a gag in his mouth, naked but for his boots. Misty/Mandy mumbled the incantations in a role reversal from when they were youngsters.

They were trying to conjure his soul from his body. Crimson/Candy wanted to capture a soul in a jar, saving it as a special gift for some imperious fop in the future, once they started to save or avenge other women.

Misty/Mandy merely wanted to *see* someone's soul, imagining it might look like a smoky ghost. But she likewise figured they weren't choosy enough with their victims, and believed they was handicapped without her blood courses. Rueful in the firelight, Misty/Mandy surveyed her flat chest under her country vest: no blood moons meant no breasts neither. She was distracted by her miniature nubs until Crimson/Candy cried in disgust, "Failed again! What do we do with him?"

Another failure meant thwarting her twin, providing slight satisfaction for Misty/Mandy. *If Mama only knew how cruel her favored Crimson was, she'd be in for a dose of reality!*

They released the young man, eyes as big as bowls and bleeding arms, with a stern warning to keep his trap shut. After they returned to their cozy, multi-storied, clapboard house with the charming turret at the end of the best cobblestone lane in town, Misty/Mandy discovered new blood in her panties!

She was overjoyed that her blood moons had come, and tonight Mama clapped for her alone. Now Crimson/Candy wore the shadowy look of envy. Big Brother Georgie, for whom their mother had such high hopes, snorted in contempt, enough to draw the girls' cool consideration.

"Georgie Porgie," they whispered in his ear at night while he slept; two fledgling monsters.

***

They may not have started their blood moons together, but they reached menopause during the same month forty-five years later. The aging twins were more skittery anyway, especially Crimson, but menopause caused them to sink in depression and night sweats. Misty's ovaries woke up once in a while to say hello, and they *stung.* Crimson wept copiously for no reason, hiding in her suite in the seaside cottage for a week at a time, before emerging with a bright, insane smile.

Driven away from the village by howling neighbors — with their mother's bags of silver and

most of the furniture — they'd fled with Georgie
Porgie too. In their late thirties by then, spinsters, and
Mama already gone, perished from some ailment
immedicable to either the local leech with his physic
medicines or to the twins' magical cures. To Misty,
the most important possession was Mama's money
(Old Papa had been rich, croaking a week after they
was born, so the girls never knew him). But to
Crimson, the most precious item was the porcelain jar
with a snug lid holding Georgie Porgie's soul.

They had discovered it was family blood,
combined with both menstruating girls that mattered
most in conjuring. Certainly, Georgie Porgie wasn't
the same after he lost his soul, a rambling moron with
a dullard's eyes and a brand-new expression of
perpetual fishiness, or distrust, earning him his
humiliating double name in the family tradition. He
crushed his Mama's spirit with his witlessness. She
never knew what the devil happened to him, her
favorite theory being a high fever she missed. Georgie
Porgie obeyed orders, though, and his brawn
remained useful to the women.

After four months of suffering the end of their
blood moons and the enfeeblement of their magic, a
fine summer morning dawned. Misty awoke to a blue,
calm sea on the horizon from her windows, in her
spacious bedroom with a stuffed chair in the corner
and many bookshelves, to a brand-new blood course.
Whistling, she searched her linen closet for a
menstrual cloth, pinning it in freshly laundered
undies, and then with a bounce in her step, descended
the stairs to the kitchen.

She was the cook, mostly because she'd starve

if she wasn't. Georgie did chores or repairs if told how to, chopping all the wood the cottage fireplaces and kitchen ovens required. Misty lit the mess of small logs, sticks and dried seaweed waiting inside the iron stove, putting a dab of lard in the heftiest iron pan afore she cracked a dozen eggs in it, which she set above the cook flames. Skewering slabs of bread on the prongs of the iron toaster stand, she thrust it into the regular, slightly smoking fireplace in the bricked kitchen wall, keeping an eye on the sizzling eggs beside her. Bread toasted, she dropped them on a waiting platter and returned to scramble the eggs, stirring in copious amounts of black and red pepper and chopped green onions.

Busy and for once, happy, she fetched leftover ham from the cold box, artfully creating new slices with the sharp kitchen hatchet. Heating a second pan, she added the ham in order to fry it.

A light step behind her and a lighter voice, "Sister! A miracle!"

Crimson, still lovely as an older woman with her slim hips, dark blue dress immaculate if simple, with fine slippers on her feet. She never did anything, not in her whole life — except keep Georgie Porgie's soul jar secure either in her pocket or on her nightstand when she slumbered.

Misty recognized her alacrity. "You, too? It's a body function, not a miracle. I agree 'tis a goodly surprise. Call Georgie down, Sister."

"He's on the stairs, can you not hear him? Methinks you're going deaf," Crimson said, seating herself prim and proper, and drawing her fresh cloth napkin from the silverware place setting. She unfolded it tediously, spreading it out on her lap as Georgie clomped into the kitchen dining area with his work shoes untied.

To Misty's astonishment, Crimson said, "Here, Georgie Porgie. Your pants are undone." He stood before her, and the grand lady of the household buttoned up his pants. "Tuck your shirt in, dearest. Bend over and tie your shoes, too," Crimson advised him, when usually, she ignored him. "Now sit. Pour yourself a glass of plum juice, lad. While you wait for your food, you will drink it."

This is how it was with Georgie after they stole his soul. He managed to wake up on his own, and use the toilet when the urges struck, but Misty bathed him each night in his bathroom tub, rubbing him dry before she pulled his nightshirts over his head. He was docile and puzzled, easy to control, and yet required a serious amount of effort too.

As tea brewed, Crimson said, "We wanted to defend women when we were children, remember? When you were Mandy, and I was Candy?" Misty nodded, and her sister talked. "We never became the witches we thought we would be, nor the healers Mama expected. We've no family but the three of us, there are no children or husbands to brighten our days."

"Heaven's sake!" Misty was annoyed by the diatribe. "What is your point, Sister?"

"My point is that we've wasted our powers, and our lives, Misty. But we can remedy it."

"Who says I want to?" Misty demanded, picking up one of Mother's white china dinner plates decorated by purple flowers around the rims, and filling it with eggs, toast, and ham. She served her siblings with a grudge.

"This may be our last blood course, perhaps our final day," Crimson said. "Georgie Porgie, pick up your fork and eat your eggs. While our blood flows, I believe we can reverse the spell and restore his soul to him."

"Why?" Misty asked, plumping down at Mother's long table, packed and sent forth upon the road ahead of them before their birth-village stirred themselves enough to make good on their unpleasant threats to the two witches and their lumbering brother. "He'll be angry, won't he? We've wasted his life, too."

"Because we owe him."

***

That evening before his usual bath and bed, the witches drew Georgie Porgie's soul out from the open jar. By candlelight, it hung still in the air of the darkened kitchen above Mama's table, and Misty fancied it was identical to the smoky ghost she imagined as a teenaged girl. In daylight, of course, it was more like sludge, bulky and bloody too. Misty hated it.

Working together, the crones shoved it at Georgie Porgie, and when it impacted against him, it knocked his chair backward to the wood floor. Crimson with her eager expression, and Misty who was pensive, hurried to see what happened. They witnessed his soul entering his body, disappearing into Georgie like water.

Misty helped him to his feet. "All right there, old fella?"

He stared down at her, swaying a bit, then ever so slowly turned his head toward Crimson. He was their elder in reality, with gray in his hair and beard. He still couldn't speak, and Misty saw the dismay on Crimson's lovely, tired face.

"Give him time," Misty suggested as she pulled him out of the kitchen toward the stairs to take him up to his bath and bed. "Crimson? Clean up the mess for once, lazy cunt."

***

When Georgie Porgie thumped down the stairs the next morning, Crimson was seated behind Misty as usual, waiting to be waited upon. They had just finished a discussion about how their blood course (and their magic) had dried-up again overnight, Crimson grateful that they acted in the nick of time regarding Georgie's soul. Misty remained skeptical, aware of the implications of magic vanishing from their bones, of their powerlessness. Now, she heard Crimson say with gladness, "Good day, Georgie! How are you?"

Misty was familiar with the sounds of violence, the cries of a tortured boy, and the rumbling noises of an angry mob, but this was somehow more like her own.

Crimson banged her hands on the table as if she were helpless. It seemed to take *minutes* for Misty to turn around from her customary pan of eggs, feeling the chokehold, the terrible pressure on her sister's throat. Once she faced them, she watched Georgie strangling her twin sister from behind. Before she could do or say anything, he groped at a handy knife for cutting ham slices, and thrust the blade to the hilt in Crimson's heaving chest. Blood burst from Crimson's mouth, and she crumpled off her chair.

Misty felt shock, hatred, even a bit heartsick as Georgie strode around the end of Mama's dining table. *He's comin' for me.* She groped for her cook's hatchet, and found it too.

Misty smiled at him as he loomed in front of her, this vengeful giant with shining eyes full of comprehension. She used her toothiest smile, and said, "Oh, I see! This morning you want jiffy cakes instead, right Georgie?"

TROUBLE IN ROOM EIGHT
E.F. Schraeder

- For T.H.

No information on this website should be used to replace medical advice. Before altering diet, lifestyle, or behavior, talk to a medical processional. To add comments or contribute to our informational resources, please sign in or sign up for YourMed's e-news. We value your privacy and look forward to hearing from our readers. While individual variations are predictable, some common possible symptoms may include:

1. Insomnia, restless sleep, or inability to sleep through the night
2. Mood swings, unpredictable emotional reactions
3. Hot flashes, difficulty regulating internal body temperature
4. Clouded thinking, blurring thoughts, or noticeable changes in thinking patterns

5. Increased facial or bodily hair, including subtle changes to hair texture, location, quantity, or appearance

6. Fluctuations to voice, usually deepening and dropping, or scratchiness to tone

7. Increased sensitivity to sound and light

8. Detectable changes in sexual arousal levels, both increases and decreases reported

9. Decreased libido, unexpected change in sex drive

10. Variations to skin texture, especially near new hair growth, like itchiness or dryness.

***

Dryness or libido drops? Definitely not. Wetter, maybe. Heightened arousal, for sure. Some of the symptoms were accurate, though.

Structurally, my brain felt like it was un-mapping itself, hyperlinking. Like a million neurons firing at once, vibrating in a new syndicate. Come to think of it, I'd never felt my brain before. Nothing quite suggested nerves on that idiotic symptom list, unless I counted restlessness. I'd noticed changes for a while but not how I expected. Like wanting things I never wanted before.

Not wanted. Hungered. My body raved for them. Cravings tore at me. Blended my thoughts together into a woven thing until I couldn't see straight.

Something moved with vengeance and certainty. Alive. Empowered. Awake. Any metaphor like that worked. Even anger felt fresh, vital. This didn't feel like the autumn of life, but a blossoming, warm spring.

Most of all, I wanted her. Here's when it started.

***

"It started when?" Alexis frowned, pressing the phone up with her shoulder while stirring pancake batter with one hand. "Thanks for letting me know, Levi."

The bell on the door jingled as another guest entered the small dining area. Six chrome-legged tables filled the space, with inky blue tabletops that matched the vinyl padded seats. When Alexis inherited the Wayside Inn from Lucy, she fully restored it to retro glory; the project was a labor of love and welcome change of pace. Everything had been refurbished and color coordinated, circa 1957. Besides, the Wayside was a nice way to honor Lucy's memory. After her mom died, Lucy was the last family she had.

Framed old town maps and original motel postcards dotted the walls, alongside some kitsch kitchenware. Within six months, the placed looked clean and fresh. Better than it had in years.

A tall, lean elderly man scratched at an unkempt white beard and plopped into a corner booth meant for four. He turned up the coffee mug, avoiding eye contact.

Alexis bristled, but smiled. *Business first.* She ran through the names of the guests in her head.

Room eight, late check in last night. Mr. Hanosh. Ever the hostess, Alexis waved, but he ignored her. Something about him bothered her. She bit down on her lip too hard, tasted blood.

Unpredictable mood swings, indeed.

The old man peered up at her, quick. Like he smelled something. His dark eyes narrowed, nostrils flaring. Still scratching those whiskers with one hand.

Alexis turned from him. She grabbed the phone as it slipped from her shoulder and focused on ending the call. "I've got to get back to breakfast guests, Levi. I'll get on that fence today, okay?"

Upset neighbors. Gossip. Endless interruptions. Weird guests. She looked around the small dining room, cups and saucers clanking. Every noise seemed amplified. It was too early in the morning to feel this done.

Agitation stung every nerve, burning from the inside out. More than a hot flash. An electric pulse rippled through her until she wanted to jump from her skin. Muscles scalded against bones, brain sizzling with white hot rage. Every sound scraped nerves, threatened her stability.

What is wrong with me?

Levi coughed into the phone.

Alexis recoiled from the wet sound bursting into her sensitive ears. The day was already unnerving. Maybe it was the restless sleep?

Levi said, "I appreciate that, Allie. You know, I hate to complain after all these years..."

Alexis turned her back to the diner, rolled her eyes. She hated being called Allie. Her face flushed. She took a deep, controlled breath, then cut him off. "Don't worry, Levi. Really. I'm glad you called. Talk to you soon. Bye now."

Alexis hung up and pushed some straggling hair beneath her floppy white chef's cap. *Damn it'd been growing fast lately.* Like the weeds outside, everything started to feel like too much. *How'd Lucy do it all those years?* Her heart sank a little, missing Lucy. If only she could offer some advice. *Or help with the damn pancakes.*

Lucy would've made a joke about menopause and moved on. Mood swings, insomnia, and migraines. *Had to be. Wish I could be as tough as that old lady.* She took a long, deep breath, concentrating to get through the morning's tasks without screaming at anyone. Breakfast for the guests, cleaning.

But Levi's call nagged at her. If he complained to her, he was blabbing around town. *Big mouth.* Locals would talk for twenty minutes about nothing. Mornings were not an easy time for a neighborly chat, with guests dropping in for coffee at all hours. No matter what the sign said, Alexis cooked until ten, then cleaned until the early afternoon. She couldn't remember the last time she enjoyed a cup of coffee without interruption.

The inn sat twelve miles outside of Plainfield, New Hampshire. A quaint throwback with nine small white cottages with green shutters and a diner on the front of the house where guests could enjoy a full breakfast or a hot drink for the road.

Alexis put on another pot of coffee and tightened the strings of the Wayside apron over her jeans and gray fleece sweatshirt, prepping for battle. One hand wavered over the grill, checking for heat. Nothing to rival what she felt from the inside.

The bell clanged, announcing another guest. Alexis ignored her growling stomach. It'd be two hours before she paused for a slice of toast or a break.

***

"A break is what I need. We're not the Marriott, you know. There's no concierge, no 24-hour room service. No airport shuttle. There's just me." Alexis laughed. She slipped out of her apron and hung it on a hook in the kitchen.

"Well, not to suggest a conspiracy or anything, but are you sure Levi is right?" Dana asked. She cocked her head, blinking. A wavy sprig of unruly black hair fell over one eye. "How many dogs would it take to cause that kind of — nightly ruckus?"

Alexis laughed. "I haven't heard anything. Not a peep. And I haven't slept through a night in weeks. Damned menopause."

Dana nodded. "Besides, it's not like the Wayside is flush with dogs every night. I mean, geez. It's only the nine rooms."

"I know. That's what I was thinking. And I've allowed dogs here for years. Besides, I've never once noticed the noise Levi's talking about. You'd think I would've been the first." Alexis shrugged.

"How many chickens has he lost?" Dana asked.

"He said just the one, but it's the noise he's complaining about."

"Right. Noise." Dana topped off their coffees. "Well, maybe he's just lonely."

"Now that, I believe." Alexis tapped on the table. "Only six months since Levi's wife passed. I don't need another thing to worry about, you know."

Dana nodded. "And we're coming into the loneliest time of year here."

"Stick season." Alexis rested her chin on her hands, and they both gazed out the window.

Wind rattled the old windows at the diner. Glancing around, Alexis noticed how blue the trim looked against the subtle flowers on the wallpaper. Vibrant. Something reflecting in the haze of sunlight, maybe. Like she'd never seen it before. Staring at the colors, her pulse quickened.

"Does the diner look different to you?"

Dana laughed, leaning back in the old aluminum chair. "It's been the same for a decade."

"It's just so bright." Alexis reached behind her and touched the window. Everything had seemed more intense lately.

Dana turned, watching Alexis run a finger down the frame. "You're getting odd in your old age." She smirked.

"Tell me about it." The hue reflected in Alexis' pale eyes. She let out a low laugh. "So about this fence you're going to help me dig —" She noticed her hands were clenched into tight fists on the table and uncoiled them deliberately.

"I knew that was coming." Dana smiled. "It's going to take another pot of coffee and some pancakes, I'll tell you that much."

"Easy pickings, Dana. You're on." Alexis smiled, but the nagging feeling that something was wrong persisted, unravelling her nerves. Something

112

new fluttered, looking at Dana. Yearning for something that was not there before.

***

"Not there!" Alexis yelled. *She can't dig there. Not after what I found. God knows what else was buried there.*

"But this makes the most sense, Al. Why not? Lucy's buried treasure?"

Alexis panicked. "No, it's just..." Her face went dark pink. Sweat poured down her stomach.

Dana stared at her, leaning on the shovel. "Can't be pipes you're worried about out here." She walked off measurements from the easternmost cottage. "See, this gives you about five hundred feet for the fence, and stays close to the back line of the property. No more loose dogs at Levi's place." She pointed with the shovel toward the cottages. "That way all the back doors lead to a single fenced spot."

Dana assumed rational explanations. Bless her. "I know. It's just...it's going to have to be smaller." Alexis swallowed hard.

Dana shrugged, then threw her arms up. "Whatever you want."

Alexis didn't really know what to do except tell the truth. "Look, I found something." Her voice was low. She bit down on her lower lip.

Dana suddenly looked serious. "Shit, Al, what? What is it?"

Alexis walked to her and knelt low to the ground, pressing a hand flat on the wet clumps of

113

grass. "A bone." She paused. "Well, bones." Her heart thumped so hard she felt it in her throat.

Dana seemed unfazed. "And?"

"Strange bones. They had deep, jagged teeth marks." Alexis looked away, toward the hillside, then covered her eyes with her hands. She felt a migraine about to flare. "God it's bright." She moved one hand up like a visor and groped in a cargo pocket with the other for her sunglasses.

"So? Lots of animals die out here."

Alexis slipped on the shades. "It felt wrong." Her lips curled in revulsion. "There's something ugly about it, those hash marks. It's like they were buried. Added to Levi's call about the weird noises, and I don't know." She stood up too quickly and caught herself, grabbing Dana's arm.

Dana glanced over the hill of the property. "You're taking this all wrong. It's probably got a pack of wild dogs or something running through. Coyotes are a problem this time of year." She patted Alexis' shoulder.

Alexis' face tightened. "Coyotes don't bury bones."

"Well, it's not your fault. The Inn's always attracted wild animals, with the dumpster out back." Dana reached toward her.

"It looked like some kind of ritualistic burial ground, something evil." Alexis backed away. She wiped a dot of sweat from her forehead just before it rolled down her cheek. Her stomach jumbled and jumped until it felt like her intestines were in knots. *Better to let it all stay buried.* But Lucy always said the truth will out, like it or not.

Alexis glanced toward the Inn. Behind number eight, the old man sat out back at a picnic table. *Hanosh.* Even his name gave her an uneasy feeling.

Hanosh faced the backyard, looking at them, not the mountains. *Watching.*

Alexis rubbed her scalp for a moment, wondering what the hell the old buzzard was up to, staring like that.

Hanosh leaned forward like he was trying to improve his view. Something about his manner set her on edge. *Hovering.* She picked up a shovel and turned away from him, but still felt him looking.

"Well then, we can put the fence here." Dana motioned about twenty feet from where she'd originally thought. "Plenty of room." She plunged the shovel deep into the heavy soil, turning it over, marking the spot for the post holes.

Alexis watched Dana work in silence. Dana's muscles outlined by the line of sweat seeping through the t-shirt. "Nice deltoids."

Dana glanced up, grinning.

Suddenly Dana fascinated her, physically. *How'd I never notice how attractive she was*? That dark, wavy hair, her long, sculpted arms. *This was not the libido change I expected.* Dana'd done dozens of projects before. Why was this any different?

They'd never dated or even joked about dating. But suddenly Dana was the hottest person on the planet. *I can't take my eyes off her.*

Desire worked fast. Alexis' attraction moved even faster, like a hard knock on the chest.

Not romance. Lust. Fierce as lightning.

115

Dana looked up after prepping for a few posts. She smiled at Alexis. "See, we'll leave your buried skeletons alone this way."

Alexis wished she hadn't said that last part. She noticed old Hanosh was still planted at the picnic table, watching while puffing on a fat cigar.

"Be right back." *Time to make nice. Move along, weirdo.*

"I see you're adding a fence," Hanosh said.

Alexis tensed. Who doesn't love when people state the obvious? "For the dog-friendly rooms. This will give them someplace to play."

"Uh-huh." He sucked on his cheek with a loud slurp, then spit off to one side. "Dogs." He chuckled.

Alexis eyed him. *What the hell was his problem?* Annoyed by the heavy smell of the cigar, she kept a few feet between her and the old man instead of joining him at the picnic table. "Thanks for enjoying that outside." She pointed at the cigar.

He nodded. "I follow the rules. Mostly."

He didn't seem to be talking about the tobacco policy. What was this old man's deal?

"Time was I stayed here every fall, years ago." He looked uphill, toward the meadow.

Toward where Alexis had found the bones. "I get the feeling you're about to give me a history lesson. Tell me, Mr. Hansosh, how many years has it been?"

"Since I been here? At least a dozen. Before the place turned hands, I guess. Right about then, exactly." He stared at her, then snubbed out the cigar in the silver-toned ashtray.

"So you knew Lucy?"

116

He nodded.

"Why'd you come back after all this time?" Alexis sat down across from him.

Hanosh smiled. "Used to be something of a retreat. I hunted. Got to know Lucy pretty well, too." He glanced away. "We liked to visit. I guess after she passed, it just didn't seem the same." He stared at Alexis. "But that's not what you asked. Why'd I come back?" He let out a faint, crackled laugh. "Back then I was a traveling salesman. Made my rounds. Enjoyed my ports in the harbor, if you will."

Alexis felt a small shiver of discomfort. She bit down on her lower lip and nodded, hoping he wasn't Lucy's lover or something. *Gross.* And if he was, she really didn't want to hear about it.

Hanosh grinned. "This inn's special. Lucy, too. Always was. My usual arrangements were for long term rentals, you know? Not the big hotel chains. Motels have privacy. Plus the views are better when you're off the beaten path." He looked out toward the mountains. "Better view of the moon. More left to the wild, you could say."

Alexis leaned away from him. "You hunted?" He seemed so interested in that spot where she'd seen the bones. *Had he buried something?*

"I was quite a hunter." Hanosh gazed out past the meadow, sucking on a long, yellowed incisor, smacking his lips.

She could tell he wasn't going to say much. "Hunting what?"

"Oh, phantoms, mostly." He laughed. He let out a loud sigh, glancing toward Dana. He had a far

117

away stare. "Things were different then, that's for sure."

"Mm." Alexis nodded. She tried to remember if Lucy ever mentioned Hanosh but couldn't recall. He wasn't exactly the kind of man who stood out in a crowd. There was definitely something about him she didn't trust and didn't like. Maybe it was the idea of him prowling around in the early morning light, shotgun in hand, while Lucy slept.

Alexis bristled. *What kind of bones were they? And if they were something he left behind, what was the deal with the teeth marks?* She wanted to know, but she wouldn't ask.

Hanosh glanced at Dana, who headed back toward the cottages, plunging the posthole digger into the soil every two feet.

"Something familiar out there?" Alexis asked.

"Oh yes." Then that tarnished, toothy grin returned. Hanosh sucked in a mouthful of air and let out a low wolf whistle. "Like coming home."

A lump formed in Alexis' throat. She couldn't explain the feeling. Too vast to hide from, too untamed. Something like night. Something like sex.

***

Sex like someone else. Like night itself, all blurred edges. Alexis drowsy with confusion, sleepless and hungry, her mind raged with need. Unfocused.

She woke with Dana beside her, asleep, in the middle of the night. Alexis' stomach jumpy, she slid close. Traced Dana's arm with one hand while the other moved lower.

118

Dana moaned. "You waking me up for something?"

"Not pancakes." Her voice a growl, lower than usual. Cool night air whispered on their skin. Dana's breath hot, moist. Hips pushing together. Fingertips wet as dew.

Night's creatures were all wild. Like first love, free and awake.

It didn't matter that I didn't know what I was doing. It mattered what we wanted.

Alexis' hands quickened, moving to Dana. She pressed her lips to Dana's neck. Nipped.

Mouths find each other in the dark. The kisses deep. Hard. Lingering.

Unexpected change in sex drive? Check.

One hand at Dana's stomach, teasing.

The middle of the night is no place to find yourself undone. It's a dream. It's her kiss. Both of them coming like daybreak.

***

Daybreak came, and Alexis walked the trail around the cottages. Up as usual too early from a restless night. Dana still in bed, asleep. Alexis' memory a little cloudy, but the highlights played well. *If this is what the change is like, I'm good.*

The night seemed peaceful enough. Whatever dogs Levi complained about, maybe it'd been solved with that simple wire fence. Could be that's all they needed, something to settle that overgrown wildness down past the meadows. She brushed a coarse stray hair behind her ears.

119

"Everything needs a trim."

Alexis surveyed the exterior of the white cottages, checking the place for litter or damage any guests could've caused overnight. She learned the hard way it was best to do that before checkout each day. As she eyed the cottages, she noticed a funny mark on one of the doors, like it'd been marred. She hoped she'd be able to wipe it off when she did the day's cleaning. She moved closer to the door, quietly, so she wouldn't startle the guest.

Room Eight. Of course. Hanosh.

Alexis crouched to see the mark more clearly. It wasn't dirt. It was a deep scratch in the door. It'd have to be patched. Alexis frowned. Then she noticed something else.

A bit of dark, dried blood flaked into the crevice of the gouge. Without thinking, Alexis put a finger to it. Touching it, she spotted a funny bit of fur stuck deep, between two splinters of wood. She felt the little knot of tan fur tickle between her fingers.

As Alexis inhaled, she picked up a strange scent lingering beneath the faint tinny blood smell. Earthy, wild. Musk. *A scent so familiar.* She pulled her finger closer and breathed in again. Then she caught herself — acting like an animal — and stopped.

That's not just fur. It's hair. My hair.

Inexplicably, she knew.

Alexis gasped, stood up, and backed away while staring at the door. Her nerves prickled. She picked up layers of a story in that door. *How?*

Despite spending the night with Dana, something had happened last night. Something else. Something she hadn't heard. Something bad.

Alexis suspected the old man Hanosh of foul play. It wasn't hard to imagine. Her heart felt like it might pound out of her chest. Somehow, he was to blame. Ever since he showed up for breakfast, lurking, his presence infected her with an inexplicable agitation.

Maybe he'd found the hair at the picnic table, done this to scare her. But why? Hunting phantoms, he said. None of it made sense. She wished Lucy had left more records of her old guests. At least the weird ones.

Frustration and confusion melted into panic. First going to bed with Dana, now this. "Whatever's going on, I'm out of control." She shivered, terrified of the man behind that door.

***

Behind that door, Hanosh knelt down, his palm opposite where Alexis' hand lingered. "And out of time," Hanosh whispered a reply.

But Alexis didn't hear him. Not yet. She hadn't come into full power. She'd only seen half of the change.

The easy half.

She didn't know what it meant to live as a wolf while human. Hearing and smelling everything. Tasting. Heightened instincts and reflexes. Sex and lust. Intensified. Everything to this poor cub was just

121

a blackout. By the next full moon, she'd be a full wolf.

For Alexis, awareness would take time. She'd learn what she was. What the change meant to her. There'd be denial first. Some anger. But then acceptance, maybe even love.

Hanosh couldn't tell her everything. She'd never understand until it happened. But the gift he'd shared with Lucy wasn't lost. Now he knew that much for sure.

Hanosh smiled, recalling how Lucy'd responded. She loved the transformation, the strength, the cravings, and hunts. No old woman, Lucy became a beast.

They raced through the meadow shedding their clothes beneath the black sky. Wet grass clumped beneath their steps as they chased prey through the hills. Bodies morphed in a tangled mass of muscle and fur, emerging then from their fragile human skin and shifting into agile wolves. "To be that young and free again."

Hanosh took a deep breath. "Just a little longer to turn. I know what you're about to be."

He nodded. So easy to spot it. The intense moods. The focus, the heat on her face. "You're one of us now, just like Lucy. Your change is coming fast, Alexis. I smelled it miles away. It was mine once, but it's yours now."

***

"Now, you're what?" Alexis stared at Hanosh.

"No, you are, Alexis. Turning feral. Uncontrollable. You feel it, that wanting in your bones and teeth. Your bite." He touched a rough patch of skin on her cheek.

She pulled away. *This man was creepy AF, but right.* Anger, hunger, sex. Hair. Everything sparked now. Electricity lived on her fingertips in a way that made her more alive than ever before. More dangerous.

"You're a wolf."

"As in howl at the moon?"

"Like Lucy, it's your new cycle. I sensed it and came back."

Alexis thought hard. Lucy said the change was impossible to control. Unpredictable. Was this what she meant? *Menopause was a real bitch.*

OLE HIGUE

Jennifer D. Adams

A strange tingling ran across my skin. It started in an undefined place and quickly spread. As the tingling migrated from core to limbs, the heat followed. Unlike any other heat I'd experienced, this heat was both physically and psychically unbearable. The compulsion to run while rending the clothing from my body, like peeling off my skin, was almost too urgent.

"Prof, are you OK?" one of my students asked as the beads of sweat dripped down my brow, and my breathing shallowed. I had to be in control. My students couldn't see evidence of this bizarre sensation enveloping my body. The sensation that I was becoming something else chased the tingling.

"I'm fine, I just need to get some water — it's dry in here. Please open a window."

I grabbed my water bottle, left my classroom, and headed towards a water fountain. The hallway was dimly lit; the fluorescent lights flickered and buzzed. I passed the water fountain and staggered into the bathroom, to the last toilet stall. Without pulling down my pants, I sat on the rim of the toilet. By now the heat was raging. My body was no longer in my control, no longer my own. I looked down at my hands. The flesh appeared to be burning away, revealing areas of deep tissue and bone. Lashing sweat became oozing, melting flesh dripping onto the bathroom floor. A clouding of consciousness disturbed my sense of reality. My head started to spin; I collapsed, pressed my forehead against the cool metal of the bathroom stall, and slowly closed my eyes.

***

Fire emanated from her womb and escaped her body into a ball of fire. The ball levitated above the woman slumped in the bathroom stall. Her brown skin had yellow undertones – a tawny gyal; her complexion and wine-coloured shoes somehow complemented one another. The tawny gyal was breathing, perhaps trying to release the unbearable heat from her body, but her efforts were futile. The ball of fire formed a femme human figure and left the woman in her misery. The tawny gyal did not know what was happening to her body, but Ole Higue knew. Ole Higue was the reason. And when Ole Higue is hungry, she overtakes the bodies of women just edging out of the bleeding years. Ole Higue was a pure, miserable white-hot flame, searing women from their insides.

To be reminded of who she was, Ole Higue gazed at the mirror. Her yellowish eyes displayed the fearful wildness of a feral street cat. She had the sharp canine teeth to match, stained a translucent brown from centuries of indulging in her favourite meal of blood. Her kinky-coily hair was disheveled and held together at the top of her head with a red string. Her skin was praline-coloured but missing in many places, exposing intricate muscle fibres, blood vessels, nerves — flesh. The exhaustion was evident; she bore centuries of epigenetic pain of lost children and fibrotic wombs. And she was hungry. The blood of young children called to her, especially the sweet purity of newborn blood. She mourned the loss of the children while also craving their blood. It was a contradicting impulse she could not control. Her grief hung from skeletal arms in the skin that once covered her body that she is now compelled to carry for eternity. She hissed at her own image, curled herself into a ball of flames and flew through the open window.

She drifted over the city and sniffed the air for a meal. She passed over towering brick apartment buildings and tree-lined streets with rows of brownstone townhouses. She was attracted to this particular area — it was a familiar place. The beat of reggae and soca pulsed from the streets below; the smells of curries and allspice emanated from kitchen windows. She was drawn here, but it would be challenging to find an infant. Not due to the lack of infants, but to the protections. These infants were well-guarded.

Her nostrils flared in an attempt to catch the scent. Through the cacophony of smells, she caught notes of the sweet-soury smell of infants. As she followed different trails to their sources, she peeked through the windows to see what she might encounter. Some babies shared the bed with their parents. Others lay in cribs or bassinets, protected by various ancestral talismans, sacred texts or jewellery on their bodies, or near where they slept. It had been a while since Ole Higue ate; she did not have the energy to engage in spiritual warfare. Not now, not when there would be a great chance of her losing

She continued to follow the trail of scents and reached another open window. In this one, she also caught whiffs of the mother's milk. A breastfed baby would make both a satisfying and nutritious meal for Ole Higue. She peered through at the small, dark nursery room. Decals of different cartoon characters decorated delicately painted lilac and teal walls. She did not see or feel the presence of other beings or any evidence of spiritual protection, so she slid through the window and crawled over to the bassinet. She gently touched the lace that decorated the outside, and savoured the pleasing milky scent on the exhaled breath of this new human. With her melting hands, she caressed the baby's thigh, feeling the red blood cells passing through the small but rapidly growing vessels. Each cell carried what she craved; smelling was the amuse bouche, the free indulgence before the cost of life. Ole Higue cradled the baby's head, picked him up, and drew his right thigh close to her mouth. The heat of her own breath returned to her face. She was about to taste the fresh blood of this new being. She closed her eyes...

"Ole Higue! Put that child down right now! G'way!"

Ole Higue looked up at a shadowy figure. Through the darkness of the room a woman appeared with her own light. She was a slender dark-skinned woman with gray eyes. Two gray plaits hung from under her white headwrap; the rest of her was draped

127

in layers of long, white petticoats. She was tall but hunched from years of enslavement on the sugar plantation. Ole Higue often encountered these old spirits in her search for a meal. These are the ones who survived the middle passage and/or the harsh and violent conditions of the tropical sugar plantations, then died from old age. Ole Higue hissed at this spirit. With the baby in one hand, she generated a ball of fire in the other and threw it at her. The woman, a long-passed ancestor of the child, caught the fire in one hand and crushed it.

Ole Higue held tight to the baby. Another spirit appeared, this time a younger male. He wore a ball cap and a basketball jersey. Draped around his neck was a gold chain with a pendant. The pendant, an ornate cross, held a picture of the child's parents — this soul in the embrace of a beautiful woman around his age.

"Granny, nevermind." He turned to the older spirit. "I got this."

He turned to Ole Higue. "This is my *child," he said as he beat his chest with each word. Where his hand landed was a dark hole, evidence of the bullet that took his life.*

"Ole Higue, you will not *take a single drop of blood from my child. Put my son* down*," he bellowed.*

Ole Higue was hungry, but she was no match for this battle. She might have attempted one ancestor. But here were two, one of them with the fury of a father unjustly killed by law enforcement just days before his baby was born. That level of protective wrath burned stronger than any fire Ole Higue could muster. She hissed at the young soul and dropped the child. She backed away through the window, and as she started to fly away, the baby let out a sharp cry. The mother and auntie rushed into the room. Ole Higue was hungry — more now that she had been so close to a meal.

Following the scent of another newborn, she flew across the alleyway and down the street to a building two blocks away. She crawled up the side of the building and peered into the window where a newborn slept in a crib. The bare walls of the room held the stench of cigarettes, and paint cracked in places. The only furniture was the old crib and a small decrepit dresser that held the baby's clothes. There was no warmth here, which meant likely little protection for this infant. Ole Higue's mouth watered. She looked around for evidence of other humans nearby, living or ancestral. Not seeing or feeling any other presence, she entered the room.

As soon as her feet hit the floor, the tapping of a dog's paws against the wooden floor broke the silence. A large, skinny dog with small eyes and sharp, pointy ears appeared in the doorway. It sniffed the air and let out a low growl. The dog's ribs poked against its skin — the fight would be minimal. With her teeth bared, Ole Higue hissed back at the animal. With a low, stalking posture, the dog approached. Ole Higue's eyes grew narrow. Again, she hissed and bared her teeth, arching her back to make herself appear larger and more threatening. The dog was not deterred. She generated a ball of fire and threw it directly at the dog. It withered to a whimper and, with a posture of defeat, backed away from the baby's room.

Ole Higue dropped to her hands and knees and inched towards the crib. The newborn still slept soundly. She had a fleeting moment of softness as she imagined that this baby was hers. She gently picked up the child and cradled her to her breast. This child was not as plump as the others. Her arms were tiny, and her body seemed to disappear into the disposable diaper. With her melted hands, Ole Higue gently touched the soft curls on the baby's head while she sniffed the soft spot at the top.

Ole Higue was hungry.

She smelled the baby's thigh. Each blood cell that passed released the sweet and sour creamy smell of newborn flesh. Although this child was not as robust as the one before, the scent of the blood was still enticing. Ole Higue opened her mouth and lowered it to the baby's thigh. Her teeth pierced the soft flesh, and blood trickled down Ole Higue's chin and the baby's thighs. Drops fell onto the dingy crib sheets.

The baby opened its mouth and yowled, and Ole Higue reflexively pressed its face against her breast. The baby struggled as Ole Higue feasted on its blood. As the flow of blood from the baby's thigh into Ole Higue's mouth slowed, the body went limp. And when Ole Higue was finished, she returned the baby to the crib, placing her hand on the baby's thigh from where she fed. The bite marks disappeared. She waved her hand over the sheet to cleanse the sheets. In that instant, Ole Higue became a ball of fire and disappeared through the window.

Ole Higue was satiated.

The cause of death would be noted as sudden

infant death syndrome. It always was in these cases.

Ole Higue flew through the air to return to the tawny gyal in the bathroom stall. She was no longer sweating, but still feeling the heat, which slowly dissipated. She breathed heavily, her face now pressed against the opposite side of the bathroom stall, seeking new coolness. Ole Higue smalled herself into a tight ball of fire and cooled to a smooth river stone. In the form of this stone, she retreated into the tawny gyal's womb.

***

My eyes drifted open, and I shivered from the dampness of my shirt. With my hands braced against the sides of the bathroom stall, I slowly stood and stumbled out. At the mirror above the sink, my reflection stared back at me. I was pale and stunned, but the heat and tingling were gone. It was as though a part of my body went on a journey of misery for a moment, leaving the other part to suffer. I raised my hands; they were whole. My body once again belonged to me. I rinsed my face with cool water and dabbed it dry with the rough, brown institutional paper towels, then put on lip balm and filled my bottle with cold water. I took a deep breath and walked down the bright hallway to return to my students.

BECOMING
Ali Seay

She'd been told if you could survive puberty you could survive menopause. Which seemed ludicrous if you thought about it. Puberty was a rip-roaring ride that had a lot of pleasant turns. Menopause was a slow slog with many unpleasant hidden trap doors to fall through.

The hot flashes being at the top of Ruby's list.

The first week of them she thought she had the flu.

She went to the doctor. How many menopause stories start with: "So I went to the doctor...?"

But she did. She went to the doctor thinking she had some weird virus that had her heating up like a Tandoor oven only to plummet into chills when her body rectified itself and realized it wasn't on fire.

While she sat there after the doctor's clinical and unfeeling pronouncement of "It's nothing. It's just menopause. You're fine," she remembered a segment on a morning show where a douchebag of a host was put under an immense weighted electric blanket meant to recreate a hot flash.

He was bitching about fifty seconds in.

"Try it all night, buddy," she muttered.

Her finger was bleeding, and she realized that when the short, squat, immensely *male* doctor had made his parting declaration and then waddled out, she'd started picking.

Picking calmed her down.

***

Richard didn't understand her tears. He didn't see what the big deal was.

"You're a woman. You knew this was coming eventually."

She stared at him, slack jawed, for a moment. Had he actually just said that?

The fork she was holding slid into his eye easily. There was minimal resistance. He didn't even scream as the burst jelly of his eyeball slid down his cheek.

He gripped her arm, and Ruby blinked. It was fine. He was fine. It had just been a moment. Heat and rage and sadness for the changes that were coming and the things she was losing.

Something neither man could understand. Not Richard and not the waddling doctor.

She tossed the fork in the sink and muttered, "It just makes me sad is all."

That was, in fact, the understatement of the century, but what she was feeling was too big to explain to someone who didn't have an interest in understanding.

He gave her a squeeze around her increasingly rounding and squishy middle that made her wince.

Richard thought he was being supportive, but

133

he was strictly highlighting one of the things she hated most about herself right now. She hated most things lately.

He wandered off to the living room, and she made a giant salad for dinner. To try and battle the softening middle.

Ruby tried to make herself feel better. She tried a mantra like all the Instagram gurus, clean eaters, Buddha studiers, and positive thinkers online.

"I'm becoming something new," she breathed as anxiety crawled through her. "I'm transforming. I'm fine. I'm good. I'm worthy."

***

The first time she cranked up the heat it was instinct. Something she had stopped questioning lately. Richard was at work, and she was at home working on a stack of papers to grade. The heat came as it always did — overwhelming and sudden.

It creeped up her neck and then her cheeks. She could feel it being reflected back to her body by her t-shirt. It was December, and the house was a cool 67. She had threatened to break all Richard's fingers if he turned it up. He could put on a god damn sweater.

He'd given her a funny look but had indeed put on a sweater.

The hot flash happened to coincide with the heat coming on per its program. Five o'clock it cut on if the temperature was below 70, which now it always was.

Her scalp felt too tight, her thighs too plump,

her face a hot mask. She wiped the sweat off her upper lip and stared at the papers.

The rage was a thing now, too. Not just crying. Crying was bad enough, but anger, true and crystalline anger, was something with which she had to grapple.

The unfairness of it all had her jaw locked tight like a seized-up engine. First you had to go through puberty and deal with your burgeoning body and male attention — wanted or otherwise. Then you got to have babies, if you went that route. You got to watch your body, once yours and yours alone, expand and morph and accommodate another being. A parasite, basically. Then you had the privilege of pushing that parasite out through an escape hatch that could have only been designed by a man.

Then your body was truly not yours any more. Unrecognizable, and — possibly, depending on who you were — the source of food for that growing baby.

Now this. The slow demise of beauty and youth and —

"Sanity!" she barked, slamming her hand down on the stack of papers.

That was nothing compared with what she wanted to do. Ruby wanted to cut them up, tear them, toss them, maybe set a few on fire.

She put her head down, trying very hard to get herself under control. "I'm becoming something new...I'm becoming something new..."

She murmured it like a prayer. A desperate plea to anything that might be listening.

"I'm becoming something new."

She stood and walked to the thermostat.

Instead of cutting it off the way she normally did when it turned on automatically, she turned it up.

69...72...79...

She cocked her head, considering it. Sweat rolled down the hollow of her spine beneath her tee. She picked her cuticle until blood flowed, staring at the digital readout.

Finally, she shrugged, and hit the button over and over again until the projected temperature read 94.

She was afraid to go beyond that. Unsure of what would happen to their ancient radiators.

"Woman killed in boiler explosion, news at eleven," she whispered.

Then she laughed. Imagining a fiery violent death was almost comforting.

She really needed to get more sleep.

***

"Good God, Ruby!"

When he walked in the house, his glasses steamed up.

Richard couldn't shuck his coat fast enough. He dropped it on the sofa, marched over to the thermostat, and barked, "Is it stuck? Broken?"

"No," she said, putting a sloppy A on the top of a paper about *Beowulf*. "I need it."

He froze, staring at her with his mouth unhinged. "Need it? You've been threatening to skin me for weeks if I turned it up. Now it's damn near a hundred in here!"

"I'm switching tactics," she said, pulling a

136

piece from her cuticle.

She studied it. Fresh raw skin underneath. New flesh.

He turned the heat off. She heard it click.

"Richard —"

"Don't! It'll be hot in here for hours. Hours! God damn it, look at the wine."

He went off cursing and grumbling. She studied the wine as he'd suggested. Nestled together on their intricate rack. Each one bled a thin line of red from beneath its cork. The heat had compromised them. They were probably ruined. Their important juices rupturing, only to eventually dry up.

"I know how you feel," she said with great commiseration.

***

There was a time when she'd been young and beautiful and figuring out who she was. She'd met Richard and loved him. He had loved her. He'd always treated her well. Always treated her as important. Never cheated, never neglected, never abused.

They'd built a life. Had a child. Sent her off to college. They were a good match.

But sometimes he just didn't understand. Ruby had taken this as a fact of marriage. Of a long life together. Sometimes he wouldn't understand. Just like she didn't understand polishing and fondling an old car for hours only to drive it twice a week around the neighborhood like an octogenarian reliving a former glory.

If you loved someone you let them be who they were, though, right?

Right?

Richard couldn't stop her when it was the middle of the night and he was sawing logs. Ruby couldn't remember what sawing logs was like. Now she fell asleep — crashed hard is more like it — for about two hours, then she got hot. She tossed, turned, got comfortable, then was suddenly frozen and chilled to the bone from being exposed and sweating. Then she covered up and started the whole process again.

Best to embrace the experience. Welcome the heat.

What was it Bukowski said? What matters most is how well you walk through the fire. Yes. That was it.

Ruby decided, staring at the dark ceiling, that if she couldn't avoid it, she would rule it.

She got up quietly, thumbed on the bedroom thermostat. It was baseboard heat, separate from the rest of the house. She slid the bar all the way up and listened to the cold metal along the base of the walls tick and pop to life.

Then she crawled into bed next to her snoring husband, swaddled herself in the many blankets of their marital bed. She built herself a thick hot cocoon and lay there sweating. Eventually, she fell asleep. Or maybe she passed out.

In the end, it really wouldn't matter.

***

Richard was unwinding her. "Jesus Christ, Ruby. I

don't know what's going on with you."

Her hair was slicked down to her head, her skin held a skim of pooled sweat as if her layers were separating.

That made her laugh. He looked at her curiously.

"Is this all part of it?" he asked, dropping the soaking wet sheet on the bedroom floor.

He wiped her off with a dry cloth.

It made her think of when they were young and he was gallant. She started to cry.

"It?" she asked.

He looked worried and confused. He wiped her tears with a different towel. "Honey, come on. It's okay. I mean, is this part of menopause?"

"Night sweats, dizziness, excessive facial or body hair, weight gain, hair loss, joint pain, headache, digestion disturbances, and a partridge in a pear tree!" she sang.

More laughter from her.

Another frown from him.

"Sit up," he said. He held out his hand and she did, kicking the sticky comforter off her.

The room was a sweat box despite the fact that outside their bedroom window snow drifted down like someone else's dream.

"Come down for coffee," he said.

He left her there, muttering to himself as he left.

She picked at a spot on her knee. She picked it until it bled and what looked like pretty pink skin winked at her from beneath.

She was becoming something new. Something

better. Stronger, wiser.

It was fine.

She took a shower — as hot as she could stand it — and reported for coffee as requested.

At the kitchen table he watched her like she was a venomous snake who might strike at any moment.

Maybe she was.

"I'm worried about you."

"I'm fine."

"You're cooking us out of the fucking house."

"It's winter."

"Yes, it's winter. We'll put the heat on, oh...seventy-two degrees, not ninety something."

Ruby shrugged.

"Look, I know that depression and anxiety and some mental —"

She stared at him, daring him to say it. He thought she was crazy, when actually there was clarity coming. As if her body and its newly found heat were burning away all the lies, bullshit, and false narratives she'd battled all these years.

"Mental?" she prodded.

He seemed to fizzle. "Difficulties," he muttered. The best he could come up with.

"Mm-hmm. Mental difficulties. Because of my uterus."

He blanched.

"I feel fine, Richard. I haven't felt this good in years."

It was true, she realized.

Now that she wasn't fighting herself or the process, she was feeling fierce.

140

She stood, took off all her clothes, and turned the heat back up. Let him fight her. She needed this, and for once she would listen to her own needs before others.

She picked a piece of skin off her thigh. Beneath, pink skin sparkled, and a flicker of flame glowed. Was she crazy? Maybe. Was she scared of it?

No.

***

Richard started hanging out at the Fraternal Order of Police hall with his friends more. He didn't want to fight her. She knew he loved her. But he was at a loss for how to coexist with her right now.

He had left her to her own devices to figure herself out, which in a way Ruby found profoundly admirable.

As a man, he could have tried to commandeer everything. He could have ordered and yelled, or like some gothic novel hauled her off to the local mental health facility and tried to have her committed.

Instead, he kept his distance, kissed her sweaty forehead, told her he loved her and wanted to help if he could, and the one night, when her lust came on thick and raging, he laid under her and let her do her thing until she came twice.

He was a good man.

She had the oven on along with the heat. She simmered a big pot of soup on the burner. It was a whole chicken with vegetables. The whole chicken because she'd read that collagen was good for her joints now that she was of a certain age.

141

Of a certain age.

Sweat rolled off her face, down the ladder of her spine. Her armpits were rivers, her pussy felt like it was literally on fire.

Condensation trickled down the kitchen windows. She'd have to ask Richard to find out if they needed new ones. Were the seals shot on these? Or was it just a matter of the extreme between cold Vermont winter outside and balmy beach weather inside.

She pulled off her robe and walked around naked. Naked, the heat wasn't terrible. Naked, the heat felt empowering. Like she might suddenly develop a superpower.

She ate the soup at the table. All of it. The whole entire pot. Then she opened a bottle of wine.

It hit her harder than she expected. She'd read that tolerance could lower during the process of menopause. Another fun fucking fact.

"I can't even drink like I used to, apparently," she said to the chicken carcass.

Ruby spotted the wishbone and pulled it out. It splintered on one end, and she sighed — but then realized what a good picking tool that end would be.

She hadn't been able to stop picking since this all began. Sometimes the heat made it better. Sometimes the heat made it worse.

"Itching," she said to herself. "Itching is on the list of possible things to suffer during *the change*."

The sharp end of the bone slid beneath the thin skin of her wrist. Right above where her pulse thumped merrily. What was under there? What was inside the new her?

Ruby watched as a long line of glowing liquid slid from her.

"Beautiful."

And it was. An electric red with undertones of yellow. The colors matched how she felt. The colors were hers. The colors *were* her.

She slid the bone down the landscape of her forearm. More liquid, no pain.

The heat rumbled as it shut off.

She looked at it: 97 degrees on the little screen.

She clicked the button to turn it up, and the thermostat didn't respond.

Ruby went to the basement and into the back room. She turned on the light. The float in the oil tank gauge mocked her, floating at empty.

Empty.

"That's fine. No worries."

She trudged upstairs, leaving what looked like a lava slick as she walked. She smelled the rug smoking where her new juices dripped.

She wasn't a husk after all.

She built a fire in the living room fireplace. Stacked wood high the way Richard had showed her. Used kindling. Watched it catch and flare. She wrapped herself in the thick blankets stacked by the sofa.

Back when she could get cold, Rich would roll her up in one, laughing all the while. He'd call her his little burrito as he bundled her up and built her a fire. They'd watch a movie and snuggle.

Now if he touched her in bed, she'd wake him up and hiss, "Your leg is on my side."

143

It made her feel bad. She loved him.

Ruby sat right at the hearth and watched the fire burn. Under her skin something seemed to flick and dance in time with the flames. An internal mimic.

A crackling sensation rolled through her. Her head felt clearer than it had in years. Her joints didn't ache, and she felt as though she'd slept like a baby.

Ruby rocked back and forth, singing to herself, feeling what was inside her respond to what was before her.

Smoke drifted from beneath the blankets. An acrid smell of burning synthetic fibers. Then a flame licking at the edge of one of the layers. A spark. Another flame and then its twin appeared. Soon the smell of burning plastic and unnatural material.

Ruby rocked and sang and listened to her blood dance.

When the blankets had burned away, she watched her skin ripple and rupture. Watched the fire consume the *her* there used to be.

The front door suddenly flew open. Richard stark and staring with her name on his tongue, about to call out to her. Then seeing her in the firelight. In her own light.

"Ruby! Honey! What..."

"Richard." Her voice crackled and popped like a dry stump in a campfire.

He realized she wasn't burning. He realized she wasn't screaming. He realized, finally, that she had transformed.

"Ruby. What...what have you become?" he cried, eyes wide.

She loved him. Loved him so. When she was

what she had been — and now that she was what she'd become. She loved him still.

The heat that encompassed her made the air around her arm shimmer and dance. She reached out for him. "Let me show you."

SOME SAY THE WORLD WILL END IN FIRE
Jude Reid

"It all comes down to how well the treatment works," my oncologist tells me. "It's only your second injection, Carline. With a good response, we could be looking at a time-scale of, well. Many months."

I've heard the same before, except she used to say "years."

Don't get me wrong: I'm fond of Dr. Cook. We met before my first dose of chemo, back when we were treating the breast cancer to cure it, not just to slow my inevitable decline. I've gotten to know her pretty well over the years. It's not her fault nothing's worked. Not her fault I'm dying.

"How's your pain?"

I shift experimentally in my chair. My left hip isn't sore — not exactly — but I'm aware of it the same way I'd be aware of a loose tooth, that sensation of something not quite as it should be. "No worse than last time."

"We'll get you in at the start of next week for some radiotherapy. That should improve things." Her pen scratches on the paper again. It's always a fountain pen she uses, nothing flashy, either a cheap

Lamy or a low-end metal Kaweco. I make a mental note to have my secretary pick her up something decent, have it engraved with her name and qualifications. Something nice to remember me by.

"Any side effects after the first dose?"

That makes me laugh. Headaches, mood swings, dry eyes, insomnia, loss of libido — a grim procession that arrived exactly as advertised in the trial literature, only twice as frequent and four times as bad. Nothing compared to the hot flushes. One moment I'd be as close to normal as it ever gets these days, the next a furnace-blast of heat would sweep up my chest, my face burning, heart pounding, clothes plastered to my skin with sweat.

"Let's say it's the full early menopausal experience and leave it at that, shall we?"

It's Dr. Cook's turn to laugh. That's good. I don't want her taking this too seriously. A job like hers is bound to grind you down, and it's not her that's dying. "As long as you're managing it. How's your husband? Is he looking after you?"

"He's fine." I shrug. "He's coping."

I've got no idea if James is coping or not. It's been a while since there was anything remotely resembling communication at home, but if I'm honest, it's not a problem I have the time or energy to solve right now. Looking down the barrel of a metaphorical shotgun clears the mind beautifully when it comes to priorities.

"I know it's not easy, but I hope you're managing some time to connect."

I stand, my hip registering a mild objection as it takes my weight. "I think that's everything for today, Dr. Cook."

She walks me to the door of the clinic room. It's bright and airy, the pale blue walls decorated with tasteful prints of water lilies and willow trees, a photo of her smiling wife and daughters on the desk.

"I'll call you with your scan result when I have it. Hopefully we'll see some improvement this time."

"Hopefully."

I close the door behind me and walk out through the sterile hospital corridor. The clinic receptionist smiles at me as I pass. So does the nurse in the corridor. I know them all by name.

I admire Dr. Cook's optimism, I really do, but I know what the scan's going to show. Progression. Grains of rice that become knots that become tumours the size of my fist, gnawing me away one organ and bone at a time.

**

The hot flush hits just as I get into the car. I've got long enough to open the window and turn on the air conditioning, then the kettle inside me boils over and I'm bubbling with scalding heat. For half a minute I sit there, gasping and shaking, the grey Mercedes my own personal sweat-box, until enough time passes that I can think again. I hang my head out the window, panting like a dog on a hot day, and catch sight of myself in the wing-mirror. I look like I've run a marathon, hair plastered to my forehead, cheeks burning scarlet.

I'm not the first woman to go through this, I

tell myself, even if I am getting the worst of both worlds: impending death in my mid-forties and a chemical menopause just to put the icing on the cake. If my scan comes back worse again, I tell myself, I'll stop taking the injections. It's not like I haven't tried, but there's nothing wrong with accepting the inevitable, and I'd rather not spend my last weeks burning up from the inside out.

I'm supposed to be at the office this afternoon, but there's no real work for me to do. The senior partners were quite clear that there's a job for me there as long as I want it — clearly I've earned their gratitude as well as a small fortune during my career — but the interesting cases have all been shuffled over to lawyers with far less experience and ability. Besides, the sun's shining, and who knows how many more days like this I've got left?

I turn left onto the interstate and head out of town. Two junctions pass before I choose where I'm going, but once I see the turn-off marked *University*, the decision's made. It's Tuesday afternoon, and James will be in his office working on the Great American Novel when he should be grading essays. I've got documents for him to sign — all things that will make transferring the estate into his name much easier when it's time for my inevitable demise. Afterward we can go for a walk, get lunch from the cafeteria, and eat it in the quadrangle. He'll probably moan about needing to get back to work, of course, but he can spare me an hour away from his desk. Maybe we'll talk. Maybe Dr. Cook's right, and this can be our chance for a fleeting moment of connection after all.

Gravel crunches under my wheels as I drive up the tree-lined boulevard to Wellington College. It's not exactly Ivy League, but you've got to give them points for trying. The buildings are tasteful red sandstone and the extensive grounds well-maintained, even if it looks more like a country-club than an ancient seat of learning. James teaches English in exchange for a below-average salary, and Wellington in turn are happy to overlook his somewhat patchy employment history and alternating enthusiasm for alcohol and the AA.

It's blessedly cool inside the building, full of the smell of old books and locker rooms that schools and colleges buy in aerosol cans. James has his office on the second floor, between plaster busts of Walt Whitman and Robert Frost too chipped and dingy to put on the lower levels where someone might actually see them. I stop outside the door marked *Professor J. Strickland*, raise my hand to knock — and stop.

James is inside, talking to someone — a student, I guess. She sounds young, whoever she is, and suddenly I don't want an impromptu afternoon date in the quad or an overpriced sandwich in a brown paper bag. A soft little giggle comes through the door. James laughs too, followed by a few words in what I think of as his *Dead Poets Society* voice — mellifluous, authoritative, smooth, pretentious. It seems to be having the desired effect, too.

My reflection glares back at me from the polished nameplate on the door. I bite my tongue, raise my hand and knock sharply.

"Shit," he whispers, then, louder: "Hold on a moment."

"Don't trouble yourself, James."

"Shit!" he says again. The Robin Williams impression is gone, swept away by a note of panic that I haven't heard since the time he thought he'd run over next door's dog.

I can hear him scuffling across the floor as I turn on my heel, the door opening just as I step off the bottom stair.

"Wait!" he calls after me. I keep walking, and the world lurches around me. James, in his office with a student. It doesn't take much to imagine what they were getting up to in there.

My face is burning as I stalk back across the quad, my hands clenched so tight my nails are biting half-moons into my palms, my hip keeping up an insistent nagging reminder that it should also feature on my list of concerns. I ignore it. I should be upset. I'm not.

I'm angry.

I press the key button for my Mercedes and sit in the driver's seat, hands locking tight on the wheel. It's scalding in here, hotter even than earlier, and that alone is enough to set off a flush.

That bastard. That bitch, whoever she is.

In the rear-view mirror, my face is fiery red. When I look down, smoke is rising from the steering wheel in two black columns.

"Shit!" I pull my hands free, dragging fine tendrils of melting black plastic with them. "Shit!" I shove the driver's door open, and thick grey smoke billows out into the car park. One of the university porters is staring at me, and I wave a dismissive hand in his direction.

151

"Cigarette lighter caught fire!" I call, my eyes watering and my mouth thick with fumes. He squints at me, shrugs, and walks on.

Eight finger-shaped depressions are melted into the black plastic of the steering wheel. When I match my fingers to the dents, the wheel is still warm. It must have melted in the sun, the hot flush nothing but a coincidence.

It's the only explanation that makes sense.

***

As I drive home, my thoughts turn into a tangle of melted plastic as well. Maybe I got it wrong. There are hundreds of perfectly innocent reasons James might have had a student in his office with the door closed, only I can't think of any. I'm too hot, and the toothache in my hip tells me that it's been two hours since my last decent painkillers. There are some in the glove box, but if I take them I might as well pull over right now and wait for the police to arrest me for driving under the influence. I need to get home. I need some time to think.

My phone rings, and I switch it off without looking. If it's James, I don't want to talk to him, not yet.

The minutes stretch into hours before the traffic eases. The tailback behind me fades into the heat-haze as far as the eye can see. I get a vicious stab of satisfaction out of knowing that James is going to get stuck in it too. I've got the pills in my hand before the car's even stopped, and the moment the park brake goes on they're in my mouth, dry-swallowed down

152

with practiced ease. The pain eases almost instantly, back to the low, nagging throb that I've learned to live with, and my thoughts slow along with it. James with another woman. My hands so hot they melted the steering wheel.

Nothing makes sense.

I don't know what I'm looking for as I search his side of the bedroom. There's nothing in his drawers except the usual clothes and a handful of overdue credit card statements. No gift-wrapped sets of underwear for women with perky matching breasts, no little black book full of students' names, just a pile of poetry books and a copy of Nabokov's *Pale Fire*. I flick through the collected works of Walt Whitman, and a square piece of folded cardboard falls out and lands on top of the bedcover. A matchbook, the kind they give out in old-fashioned bars, even though no one smokes inside anymore.

Written in pink gel pen, in a hand so rounded and childish I half-expect to see love hearts over the letter "i," is a name — Ellie — a phone number, and a trace of floral perfume. It's hardly a smoking gun, but when it comes down to it, all evidence is circumstantial. Was it Ellie in his office, Ellie bent over his desk with her firm young body exposed, hanging on his every word, or is she just one of many?

This time the hot flush comes out of nowhere, racing across my skin with terrifying speed. The matchbook in my hand erupts into flames, and I cast it from me like a venomous snake. Flames lick into life across the bedcover. I search wildly for some way of putting it out, and fold the blanket in half to smother it. The room fills with the smell of charring hair as silk and feathers turn to ash — I fling a window open and toss the whole bundle outside into the back garden, wondering for one terrible moment if the breeze will fan it into a conflagration — but before it lands the flames have gone. I lean out, coughing and gasping, and wait for — wait for what?

The matchbook is somehow partially unburnt. Four of the matches burned down to stubs, but the last remains in its little cardboard coffin. Half of the name is gone, scorched out by the fire, leaving only L-I-E. I tuck it into my trouser pocket, then head down to the garden to clean up the mess.

My hip doesn't like the stairs much, and by the time I get to the bottom a sharpened red-hot poker is jabbing into my pelvis with every step. I dial Dr. Cook's number as I open the sliding doors and step out into the garden. The duvet lies on the ground like a murdered swan, white feathers lying in drifts by the topiary hedge.

"Dr. Cook's office."

"It's Carline Strickland. I need to talk to Dr. Cook, please."

I wedge the phone between my ear and my shoulder, and lift the trash-can lid. Mostly empty. Good.

"She's with a patient right now, Ms. Strickland, but I can ask her to call you back.

"Yes. It's urgent." What am I even going to say? The side effects are getting worse? I'm setting things on fire with my hands? "Please. As soon as she can." I swallow. "I'm having problems with the new treatment."

"I'll let her know."

She hangs up, and I turn the ringer back on. A notification tells me James has tried to call three times already. I hope the bastard's stuck in traffic. I haven't got the energy for a difficult conversation right now.

Something at the bottom of the trash can catches my eye. I lean inside, careful not to lose my balance, painfully aware of what would happen if I fell. *City Lawyer Breaks Hip, Gets Stuck In Trash Can.* I reach down and lift out one of a dozen tiny cardboard boxes, the kind that supermarkets sell Tylenol in. The blister pack inside is empty, each little white pill already punched out and used. I check another box. Identical.

I don't get it. I'm not averse to the odd Tylenol here or there, but it hasn't touched the pain for months now and I don't usually bother taking it at all — and besides, my drugs come from the pharmacy in brown plastic bottles, not colourful drugstore boxes. James is under strict instructions not to take anything likely to damage his already fragile liver — but the contents of all these empty packets would be enough to poison a whole AA meeting.

The little silver blister-strip catches the light as I turn it back and forward. White powder clings to the inside of the empty plastic pockets. I drop it back into the trash, stuff the ruined duvet on top of it, and slam the lid shut, just as my phone rings.

"Hello?"

"Carline. It's Dr. Cook."

"Oh, thank God." I walk back into the house, ignoring the flurries of white feathers that follow me in through the sliding doors. "I'm having bad side

155

effects on the new treatment. The hot flushes. They're..." I glance at the trashcan. "...pretty extreme."

"Okay." She sounds thoughtful. "We can add in some other drugs to try and manage that, if you like, but if it's that bad we should think about stopping the injections, just keep going with the tablets."

"Yes. Please. I think that's a good idea. How soon 'til the effects wear off?"

"Bear with me. I'll need to withdraw you from the trial to know exactly what you've been given." Her fingers tap out a staccato rhythm on her keyboard, and she makes a soft humming noise deep in her throat. "Okay. What side effects did you say you were having?"

"Mostly the flushes. Really hot. Like...hot enough to burn."

"Mmm." Another series of taps. "So, I've got your file up here. You're in the control arm of the study."

The words bounce off my skull. "The control arm?"

"Yes. You're not getting the active agent, the injection's a placebo. And these side effects have just started, you're saying?"

"Yes, since —" Keys rattle in the front door, and I lose my train of thought. James. It must be James at the door. "Since earlier today."

"I think we should make you another appointment, chat it through in person."

"Sure. That's fine." Sweat prickles on my forehead. "Thanks."

She's still talking as I hang up. The front door opens, and James is standing there, his face flushed as red as if he was the one having the sweats. Even at ten feet, the stink of booze is unmistakable. He must have been drinking the whole drive home.

"I can explain." He slurs the words.

"Who's Ellie?"

"What?"

"Or whatever the fuck her name is. Whatever jailbait you had in your office today."

"It's not what you think."

"Liar." I toss the matchbook at his feet. "Did you read her chapters from your masterpiece, cry on her shoulder about your dying wife? I bet that sort of bullshit plays well with Wellington girls."

"It's not like this has been easy for me!" His face is scarlet, his eyes watery like he's about to start blubbering.

I take a step towards him, and he flinches away. "For fuck's sake, James, even your adultery is derivative crap."

"Shut up!"

The slap is completely unexpected. I stumble to my right, barely feeling the sting on my cheek, and my hip chooses that moment to give way completely. A bright white pain shoots through my right side as I crumple at the foot of the stairs, grey blotches swimming in front of my eyes. I try to stand, but the grinding of bone on bone informs me that won't be happening any time soon. Cancer, unlike James, has an impeccable fucking sense of timing.

I drag myself away, inch by painful inch. My phone's just out of reach, a yard from my fingertips beneath the hall table. I need an ambulance — an ambulance and a big shot of something to take the pain away. If I call Dr. Cook, maybe she can get someone here quickly.

James steps between me and the light, picks up my phone, and puts it in his pocket. Something about his expression sends a chill down my back, fear cutting through the pain. "Honestly, Carline, you're supposed to be dead by now." The hysteria is gone from his voice, replaced with something cold and sharp I don't like. "I thought when the cancer came back that would be it, but no, there's always another treatment, something else to keep you clinging on for a few months more."

I haul myself another foot across the floor, the splintered ends of my hip-bone grinding into each other with a flare of agony that leaves me breathless and blind.

"You don't even have the good grace to die on time."

I roll onto my back. "The Tylenol." My voice is a croak, feeble and thin. I don't sound like me. "The empty packets in the trash."

"You finally worked it out, did you?" Spit flies from his mouth. A drop lands on my face, where it spits and hisses like fat on a griddle. "Turns out cheap painkillers look pretty much exactly like expensive hormone-blockers when you put them in those little brown plastic bottles. I've been doing you a favor, if you think about it — all your precious oncologist is doing is prolonging your death. And wasting my fucking money while she does it."

My gut lurches, and for a second I think I'm

going to be sick, but it's a laugh that bubbles up in my throat instead. "You're a piece of shit, James."

"Yeah?" He bends down next to me. "But in about an hour, I'll be a rich piece of shit, and I hear that makes all the difference."

I shoot a desperate look around the room, searching for a lamp, an umbrella, something I can use to shove him away. Nothing. He reaches his left hand towards my face, the afternoon sunlight glinting off his wedding ring.

"It'll all be over soon."

A decade of living with cancer has eaten most of my strength away. I flail at his face, and he jerks away, red weals rising beneath my fingers.

"Bitch!" He stands, takes a calculated backswing, and kicks me full-strength in my broken hip. Pain explodes like a supernova. I can hear someone screaming, but all I can do is float in a sea of agony until my nervous system kicks back in and I heave the contents of my stomach onto the floor.

Rough hands roll me face-up. James presses my mouth shut with one hand, pinching my nostrils closed with the other. "Lie still, Carlie."

I fumble at his wrists, but he's too strong. I fumble at the ground, trying to get enough purchase to crawl away, and my searching hand closes around the discarded matchbook. My throat's locked tight, my chest heaving in the desperate attempt to draw air into my empty lungs, the world turning grey at the edges, the afternoon sunlight hot on my skin and the sheer injustice of it all — what a fucking stupid way to die — burning like a bellyful of hot coals.

The match in my hand flares into life. I thrust

it blindly towards his eyes and he screams. The pressure on my face eases, and I suck in a welcome breath of air.

The heat in my belly is unbearable, unimaginably intense. I grab James' ankle; flame erupts from my hand and races up his trouser leg like a candle wick. He screams again and slaps at his flaming crotch — I grab his other ankle, and a fresh burst of blue-white fire leaps upward. The pain in my hip is gone, and I'm rising from the floor with my wings unfurling, towering over my husband as his hair singes and the skin of his face blisters and burns.

I draw back my head, open my muzzle, and a brilliant jet of fire surges out in a wave of shuddering pleasure a million times better than anything he ever gave me in fifteen years of marriage. Flames reflect in his horrified eyes, then he's gone, nothing left but a mess of overdone pork and crackling.

For the first time in years, I realise he smells pretty good.

I should have divorced him before it came to this, I think, as what's left of his bones crack in my new, powerful jaws. But on reflection, this is better. Much better.

FIFTY-FOUR YEAR ITCH
Shelby Dollar

Yoga mat beneath her feet, Heather fought to keep her balance while the others held their poses like herons on water, golden eye pendants glinting on their necks. Sponsors. The women were Heather's age, but they had a quiet power. A confidence that held gazes with ease. She found them fascinating and longed to be on their level.

"Stop staring," muttered Amy, Heather's sponsor.

She didn't care. Sponsors loved being watched, and so did Heather.

Heather used to despise the idea of being ornamental, a beautiful fixture for others to hang their dreams on. Her youth and beauty were something to exploit, so she longed for loneliness, and slowly, aging had given it to her. At fifty-four, she was an eyesore, an obstacle that potential partners avoided. She hated herself for it, but it gutted her. To be desired was thick in her marrow, a power she hadn't tapped into completely. She now knew how fragile it was.

"Reclaim your body, your power, and all eyes will be on you." Menolize's motto promised her aging

body would no longer be a burden but a gateway to new opportunities. She downed the four pale green pills a day but waited for disappointment, dressing in layers to prepare for the inevitable hot flash. But one never came. Instead, her skin got plumper, her joints less pained, and people stared at her like she was walking, breathing art.

The attention was like bathing in warm sunlight after a long winter, and she was convinced these pills would change her life. She became a seller and found comfort in the company's social media groups and forums, in the success stories. But she wanted more: to be a sponsor.

Heather rolled up her mat, frustration heating her face. "I've sold my weight ten times over in product," she said. "What am I doing wrong?" Amy had told her to come to this convention, promised to help her get to the next level. But so far, it was all power yoga or motivational luncheons.

"You've done wonders in recruiting." Amy stretched her bony arms. "But you're holding back, hiding."

"I'm getting out there," Heather said, anger flaring.

She was, but it was more to get her fix of that hair-raising sense of being watched. Heather would root herself at a bar or restaurant just to bask in the stares. Sure, she hadn't acted on it yet, but it just needed to be the right moment. She didn't want rejection to taint that weightless sensation forever.

Amy sighed, a recognition of the agitated air between them. "We really just need to get you laid."

***

The women descended upon the hotel bar in a flurry of floral perfume, slinky fabrics, and shimmering eye shadow. They settled into a booth, gemmed ears and hands glinting in the dim light. Heather smoothed her black dress, enjoying the slick fabric that pinched her in at all the right places and glimpsed her leg with a thigh-high slit. She used to wear this dress to boost her confidence or to get a lover in her bed before it became too disappointing, too suffocating. But tonight, it was drenched with possibility.

Drinks arrived, and Heather sipped her mint julep, savoring the burn of the whiskey. She scanned the bar, filtering out her options for how the night could end while the others laughed about a drink with champagne and pineapple juice called *Sex on the Mind.*

"Let's play a game." Amy leaned in, a smile twisting her red lips, color threatening to bleed into a gory smear. She tilted her head in Heather's direction, a challenge. "Go pick up one of those guys at the bar."

Her stomach twisted seeing the small group of men in their twenties, bodies lean and heads full of thick hair. They downed beer with ease, eyes glued to a flatscreen running a local football game. She hesitated, and Amy snapped the stem off a maraschino cherry. "I thought you were ready. Or was that all talk?"

Heather tossed back her drink and glass clinked. "Fine," she said, the words heavy on her tongue. She kept her breath steady and sauntered

163

across the bar, her thoughts circling. These weren't the men on Matchme, jaded by failed marriages, their bleary eyes lingering on women young enough to be their daughters. Life had yet to take its toll on the young group, so why would they want her? She stopped, their eyes turning from confusion to hazy delight, as if catching a warm, summer breeze.

The thread of terror in her broke, and she smiled, placing her hand on one of the men's backs. He had gray eyes flecked with green, lichen and moss on cool stone. "You've got beautiful eyes," she said, waving the bartender down.

"I don't hear that often." His voice was smooth like oil and reeked of sharp-sweet yeast, reminding her of college dorms and house parties.

She laughed. "Doubtful."

"Fine." He raised a hand in surrender. "You got me. But you get points for the compliment anyway."

Her non-question reeked of sarcasm. "Oh really?"

"Well, if you believe the cheesy saying of eyes being windows to the soul …" He swigged his beer, bottle sweating. "Then that means you got a glimpse of mine and liked it."

Heather searched his face for fault lines, indicators that the statement was a farce, but he gave none. He finished his beer and smiled. "Alright, what are we drinking?"

***

Slots of moonlight segmented the dark hotel room as

Heather's body ached for Green Eye's touch. Naked, insecurities threatened to claw their way into her. It was too intimate to reveal her curves dimpled with cellulite, her breasts heavy and drooping from years of gravity's pull. There were some parts of her that pills or yoga could never fix.

His hands explored her body, savoring her as if she were the first woman he ever touched. His mouth crashed with Heather's and the musk of him flooded her, pine needles on a damp, forest floor. Hot need pitted in her gut, spreading and swelling with his hunger for her. Consumed and wanting to burst, she moaned.

Never had she felt so loved.

Spent and tangled in damp sheets, Heather touched the supple skin of his face, committing it to memory. Head on his chest, the beat of his heart lulled her like the steady crash of the ocean. He kissed her and said they had a true connection, one worth pursing further. Heather agreed, but surely it wouldn't last. Nothing this good ever did.

"You don't mean that," she said.

He sat up. "If that's not what you want, I understand."

"No." She grabbed his hand, the words sticking in her mouth. "Stay. Please."

He settled back in, and she nestled into the crook of his arm. She breathed him in deep, listening to his heartbeat, the air between them charged with hope.

***

In the harsh light of morning, Heather woke to the slow and breathy click of the air conditioner whirring on. Clothes — including Green Eyes' — were strewn across the dingy carpet, and there was no note or soft shutting of doors to indicate a swift getaway had happened, but she was alone.

Disappointment unfurled in her chest. Green Eyes had ditched her after all.

And that's when she realized it: that suspiciously wet feeling creeping from her thighs, one she hadn't experienced since hitting menopause. Heather flipped back the comforter.

Splatters of dark blood stained the bed. She cussed. Spotting was a possible side effect of Menolize but this was excessive. She started the supplement to gain control over her body, her relationships. Not to sabotage it.

Heather gathered up the sheets before she showered, anxious to wash the previous night down the drain. Under the pattering stream of water, drops of rusty crimson flowered and swirled. She grazed her ribs and felt two swollen knots. Firm like grapes, they pricked her nerves in an irritating pleasure that begged to be touched. She raked over them again and again, regretting her decision to not wear bug spray yesterday during yoga. The mosquitos had been vicious this year.

She should leave the bites alone, the tops a weeping, angry red. But God it felt good, and every time Heather thought it would be her last, she'd drag her nails back and forth to get another fix. It was worth the moments of relief.

166

***

At breakfast, the air was sticky with the caramelized smell of fat crisping. Suffocating steam rose from gleaming lids as Menolize women glided through the buffet line with a pride Heather was devoid of. Men followed them, loyal shadows that listened intently and laughed accordingly with their older counterparts. Irritation flowed in her veins. It was foolish to think she could have that in broad daylight and not just behind closed doors.

"Successful night?" Amy said, butting into line with a blonde-haired man.

"No." Heather prodded undercooked eggs, whites a smear of mucous and reeking of iron. She didn't want Amy to know how far the night had gone, to relive the embarrassment of being good enough to screw but not enough to love.

"Really?" Amy's brows raised. "And you're taking the pills every day?"

"Yes," she said, her frustration fanning.

"What can I do to help?"

Heather's skin prickled with the brushing of a thousand tiny legs, swarming and pulsing, a constant buzz that wouldn't quiet. "Nothing." Heather scratched, relishing the reprieve.

Amy's lips twisted into a faint smile. "You sure?"

Hunger gone and shrivelled up with her patience, Heather told Amy her stomach was too sour for breakfast, that she needed to sleep it off. It was a lie, but Heather couldn't tolerate the brigade of joyful women or Amy's incessant questions. All reminded her of her failure, the gentle rattle of the Menolize pills in her purse feeling like her own personal vacancy sign.

When she got back to her room, the soiled bedding was gone, and fresh linens were in their place. She welcomed the astringent smell of the bleached sheets, relieved that there was one less hint of Green Eyes in her room. Heather snapped open a plastic laundry bag and stuffed his clothes into the sack. The sooner she got rid of him, the better. But she paused when his phone dropped out of a pocket. She could believe he slipped out of her room practically naked, but leaving his phone behind?

Heather's throat tightened, and she swallowed.

He hadn't just disappeared on *her*. There were dozens of unread messages and missed calls.

The tacky sap of the sore-ridden bumps stuck to her fingers. Feeling the bites was comforting, satisfying. A wound she had to pick.

Incoming texts flooded his phone, one after another:

> *"You still with that old bitch?"*
> *"Do I need to call police?!"*
> *"WHERE ARE YOU?!"*

THUMP! THUMP!

Pounding at the door. Room service? Heather peered through the peephole. It was Amy, her grin wide and distorted in the fisheye lens.

"Heather," she sang, fingers thrumming the door. "I know you had sex last night. Open up."

When she did, Amy fixated on Heather and

168

her scratching. "You've got the itchies." She said it with finality. "Common when you're on the pill."

Heather sighed. Amy had always been flamboyant, her personality a range of colors not contained within lines. She was never quite sure how to handle her. "What do you want?"

"To celebrate! You made sponsor."

Sponsor. It was what she wanted. To be an integral part of the Menolize community, full of mixers, conventions, and life-long, meaningful connections. But last night had planted wriggling seeds of doubt in her gut. The supplement had failed her.

She tried to seal out the disappointment in her voice. "That's all it took?"

"I know, it's a little childish." Amy tugged her out of the room. "But necessary, you'll see."

In an elevator stinking of bleach and fresh pool water, her side twitched, but this time she couldn't hold back. Heather scratched and scratched and scratched, unable to stop even as Amy sat her down in the hotel ballroom, its dizzying carpet a collage of peacock feathers with indigo spots and fingered plumes that curled like lashes on eyes.

Below the glimmering brass chandeliers, women filled the dozens of seats, some pale and exhausted, hands raking their clothes or digging into their scalps, infested with an unseen irritant. Onstage, at the front of the room, a woman tapped the mic, and a low thud-thud-thudding reverberated.

"This is your friendly reminder to please take your seats. We will shut the doors shortly." She positioned water at the podium, then sauntered down the aisle, silence blowing through the crowd.

The bumps burst, and subtle warmth bled through Heather's shirt in a splotchy trail. She stared at her hand slick with blood and struggled to form the words or come up with a solution, her nerves fraying.

With the precision of a mother tidying a child, Amy broke out a wet nap. "The first one is always a little messy," she clucked before quickly adding, "This is normal. Don't worry, it's just a little blood."

Heather nodded, but her gut didn't agree. It didn't *feel* normal. The itching was gone. But there was something else now beneath the knots, a round rolling against her ribs.

Abigail Larson, the founder of Menolize, approached the stage in a shimmering long-sleeve dress that pooled at her feet like fallen stardust, her silver and black hair pinned with dazzling barrettes. Drifting on an invisible current, she twirled and enjoyed each step with her chin tipped high. Her body wasn't perfectly toned, but strong and capable.

"Welcome," she said, her voice silk and honey. "And thank you for coming with us on this journey. I know it hasn't been easy. You've got doubts."

She bowed her head, and the woman from before unzipped Abigail's dress. "But I promised you freedom, adoration, and power — and I intend to make good on it."

This was too strange. Heather wanted to bolt. But Amy squeezed her arm, a silent warning. Abigail freed herself of the clinging fabric and stepped out of her heels. Heather's mouth turned to sandpaper, and a small cry crept out of her throat, gasps and murmurs boiling throughout the room. Hundreds of puckered lumps riddled Abigail's stomach, arms, and breasts.

This was what they promised. A hideous side effect no one had disclosed.

Abigail kept her composure, polished fingers caressing her body. Her lips parted in a sigh. "I know my absorbed lovers aren't much to look at. But..."

She threw her arms out, and all at once the hundreds of slits fluttered open. Her body bloomed into a shifting mosaic of hazel, emerald, amber, and ocean-blue eyes. They blinked and rolled, frantically glancing. "They're mine. Forever."

The mood among the women shifted. Their heads tilted with curiosity while others leaned forward to listen. Heather imagined Green Eyes nestled in her skin, a pair of brilliant jewels.

"From the moment they slip inside you, like they've done to others countless times." Abigail arched her back in bliss, the eyes lulling to sleep. "There are no more fast getaways or rejection. Just you and them..." She laughed. "And a little spotting."

Heather's skin twitched at the tickle of tiny, dense hairs fluttering together, blinking. Deep inside her, ecstasy stirred as the crowd broke into deafening applause.

Green Eyes never left, and he never would. Finally, she had control, and it was beautiful.

THIS IS YOURS
Max Turner

Sam couldn't blame the pain on the raw scar across her abdomen. It was thick and pink, but it was healing and hadn't become infected. No, they wouldn't want that. They didn't want any of them to die, only to suffer.

That thought was fleeting, as was the accompanying sense of wrongness. Of her body being wrong. Alien.

Another flash of heat winded Sam, the aching in her joints now echoing around her body. And it wasn't just the discomfort — it was the brain fog and the exhaustion. She could barely focus on where she was or how she got there.

Sam drew in a sharp breath as she realised someone stood next to her chair, situated as it was by the window onto the gardens. In her more lucid moments she was sure this was simply a screen, and she had seen the same blackbird devouring that worm time and time again.

One of the nurses silently loomed, and then there was the familiar icy feeling in her veins and she felt groggy again. At least it was some consolation that they kept her sedated so much of the time, there was less discomfort and confusion that way. Less pain.

Sam's eyelids drooped, and the wrongness drifted away.

***

"Sam? Sam?"

Sam revived to a nurse patting his hand. It seemed a warm gesture, though that warmth didn't make it as far as the nurse's eyes.

"Time to get you ready for surgery."

Sam tried to move, but restraints held him pinned to the gurney.

"Please, no," Sam groaned and shook his head. There was a darkness at the edges of everything, an intense headache. But despite the pain, he knew this wasn't right — everything was wrong. His body was racked with an intense heat spreading all over and making his face burn. Where his flesh wasn't heated, it itched, all the way down to the ends of his fingers that were tingling at the tips.

This was all so wrong. He couldn't even remember how he got here, just the pain and the discomfort. The sense of everything being so utterly out of place. Himself most of all.

He'd already had surgery, he recalled that much.

They had cut him open and put something inside him, and now he was so sick. Too hot, his joints ached, he was exhausted. It was almost unbearable. It was some sort of torture.

"Please, no more..." Sam begged.

The nurse turned away from him then, and a shadowy figure appeared. It took a moment for Sam to focus enough to see who it was. A tall man with a surgical mask; the memory of him standing over Sam before his previous surgery came to the fore.

"I shouldn't be here," Sam pleaded with the doctor, his voice trailing off as he recalled what had happened before. What this doctor had done.

Heart pounding and now struggling to breathe through the tight grip of anxiety, Sam looked down at his prone body. He had meant to seek out the abdominal scar, to try and confirm what he was starting to remember. What these monsters had done to him.

But instead his eyes focused on the dark markings on his chest. It had been shaved and a black pen used to mark out intended incisions.

"No...please..." Sam sobbed. He remembered the joy he had felt when he had been marked up like this in the past. The euphoria when he had come around from the operation to find his body more reflective of his true self.

"Don't worry," the doctor reassured in words if not in tone. "You'll be back in convalescence before you know it, Miss Blanford."

Sam screamed.

Three Weeks Earlier

The air was thick. The metallic scent of blood and overpowering citrus notes that tried to mask the bleach sat heavily at the back of Sam's throat as he stirred, bewildered as he came to. He hadn't been here

174

earlier. He had been somewhere else.

At home?

No, he had left work and was on his way home, and then someone had stopped him in the street. There were so many people there going about their business, and yet not one of them had stopped to help him.

They'd called him Miss Blanford and flashed their badges. Dread had filled him from his stomach upwards and he knew. Before he had a chance to react or even deny the identity, there was something wet across his mouth and nose, and everything went black.

"I believe this is yours." The doctor's tone was cold with a note of disgust. Beneath the surgical mask he was probably sneering. Sam couldn't look away, restrained as he was, whilst the doctor held up a pale human organ. Whilst Sam had no medical knowledge to identify it for sure; there was only one thing it could possibly be. One thing that the doctor wanted to be sure that Sam saw.

This wasn't how it was meant to be. It had been taken over a decade ago, when Sam was young and couldn't imagine a life ahead with it still inside him. He knew that he wouldn't have survived that life, that version of himself.

"Please...I don't want it," Sam tried to say, though the words came out mumbled.

"Don't trouble yourself." The doctor signalled over someone else, another masked person who began to fiddle with the IV next to Sam. "We'll soon have you back under, and the next time you wake up you'll be in our convalescence facility."

Sam felt the burn of tears rolling down his

face. He tested the restraints and found no give at all. He had heard so much about those facilities, rumours and horror stories. Conversion, brainwashing, reconditioning.

They were about to give him back something he did not want or need and take everything else from him in return. The thought was terrifying, as a sudden wave of dysphoria hit him at the memory of those painful younger days.

"I can't, not the periods, not again, please..." The words came out slurred, and his eyelids started to feel heavy.

The doctor cocked his brow and his eyes shone, and Sam knew he was grinning beneath the mask.

"At your age? Luckily for you I think those days are behind you." He continued preparing a tray at Sam's side.

"Why are you doing this?" Sam tried to cry out desperately, though once more it was muffled and ill-formed by his slackening mouth.

He already knew the answer.

That thing he had been fearing and hiding from since this government's first term in office. And now with another four years ahead of them to put into practice all those policies they had previously only threatened, they had caught up with Sam. As they would likely catch up with them all, tracing them one by one from records once held in the now-defunct Gender Clinics.

"Government orders," the doctor replied dismissively as he continued to poke and prod, though Sam could no longer feel the sensations as his lower half went numb. "All transitions to be reversed where medically possible. And, like I said, don't worry about menstruation. Given your age and the age of this donor uterus, it's likely that you will begin to experience menopausal symptoms almost immediately. Don't panic. I assure you this is quite normal."

The scream of terror in Sam's throat was nothing more than a whisper as he sank into unconsciousness.

Author Biographies

Jennifer D. Adams was born and raised in Flatbush, a Caribbean community in Brooklyn, NY. Her mother is from Jamaica, and she grew up hearing tales about Ole Higue, rolling calf, and other duppy encounters. As an academic she studies the intersections of race and learning and uses creative writing as a way to explore Caribbean cultural themes with her culture and make research more accessible and relevant to people outside of the academy. She dances, runs, does triathlons, and loves the ocean. She currently lives and works in Calgary, Alberta with her two cats Mitza and Griffin.

Megan M. Davies-Ostrom is a Canadian author with a love of long-distance running, strange cats, and horror-themed board games. Her short stories have appeared in Cosmic Horror Monthly Magazine and various anthologies, including *Brave New Girls* and *Thuggish Itch.* Her website is mdaviesostrom.com

Shelby Dollar lives in Kansas City, Missouri. Her fiction can be found in Magnificent Cowlick Media and Ghost Orchid Press. She is also a co-host for the horror podcast, *Podenstein's Lab.* When she isn't writing, she travels with her husband and hangs out with Wally, their rescue dog. Follow her on twitter @SCDwriter or visit her website at shelbydollar.wordpress.com

D. A. Jobe is a Virginia writer whose idea of a good time is curling up with a scary as hell book or watching a monster movie. Her work has appeared in national publications, including The Washington Post Magazine and Brevity. She builds a walk-through curiosity cabinet every year for Halloween and has acted as a zombie at a local haunt. She is currently working on a horror novel. Twitter: @D_A_Jobe

Joe Koch writes literary horror and surrealist trash. A Shirley Jackson Award finalist and author of *The Wingspan of Severed Hands* and *The Couvade*, their short fiction appears in *Year's Best Hardcore Horror*, *The Big Book of Blasphemy*, *Not All Monsters*, and many others. Find Koch at horrorsong.blog and on Twitter @horrorsong.

Dr. Bunny McFadden tinkers with words for a living. She's written for a variety of dreadfully boring academic publications, and has hosted workshops on storytelling with UNICEF, the University of Connecticut, the Royal Centre School of Speech and Drama in London, and the Assembly for the Teaching of English Grammar. She's also the assistant managing editor of a literary magazine for incarcerated folks. After living in Switzerland for a year, she moved to California's golden coast and enjoys contemplating the horrors of the neighboring ocean while playing with her two sandy offspring and her beta reader. Her website is DocBunny.com.

Monique Quintana is from Fresno, CA, and the author of *Cenote City* (Clash Books, 2019). Her work has appeared in Pank, Wildness, Cheap Pop, Okay Donkey, and Luna Luna Magazine, where she is a contributing editor. Yaddo, The Mineral School, the Sundress Academy of the Arts, the Community of Writers, and the Open Mouth Poetry Retreat have also supported her writing. You can find her at @quintanagothic and moniquequintana.com.

Max Turner is a gay transgender man based in the United Kingdom. He is also a parent, nerd, intersectional feminist and coffee addict. Max writes speculative and science fiction, fantasy, urban fantasy, horror, and LGBTQ+ romance, and more often than not, combinations thereof. You can find him at maxturneruk.com or on twitter @robot_tiger

Jude Reid lives in Glasgow and writes horror stories in the gaps between full-time work as a surgeon, wrangling her kids, and trying to tire out a Border Collie. In 2021 she won the Kelpies Prize for Writing, and she was commissioned to write a piece for the National Library of Scotland's Fresh Ink collection on the subject of "my experience of 2020." You can find some of her audiodrama work at www.hunterhoose.co.uk and on twitter at @squintywitch

Julie Ann Rees holds a first class Masters degree in creative writing from the University of Wales Trinity Saint David. Her short stories have been published both online at horla.org and in print with Parthian Books' *Heartland,* Black Shuck Books' *Dreamland: Other Stories* and a forthcoming anthology with Improbable Press. Her first book, a memoir entitled *Paper Horses*, will be released by Black Bee Books in October 2021. She is a single mother and works at a busy rural library in Wales. When not riding her horse over the wild Welsh hills she can be found on facebook.com/julieannrees and twitter @JulieRe36071199

Marsheila (Marcy) Rockwell is a Rhysling Award-nominated poet and the author of twelve books and dozens of poems and short stories. She is an active member of SFWA, HWA, IAMTW, and SFPA. She is also a disabled pediatric cancer and mental health awareness advocate and a reconnecting Chippewa/Métis. She lives in the Valley of the Sun with her husband, three of their five children, two rescue kitties (one from hell), and far too many books. You can find out more at marsheilarockwell.com or follow her on twitter @MarcyRockwell

Carman Webb lives and writes in North Carolina. When she is not reading or buying books, she is working on a novel set during the 2016 election. While she is notoriously bad at twitter, you are welcome to find her there @cgwebb06.

E.F. Schraeder is the author of *Liar: Memoir of a*

Haunting (Omnium Gatherum, 2021), the story collection *Ghastly Tales of Gaiety and Greed* (Omnium Gatherum, 2020), and two poetry chapbooks. Recent work has appeared in Strange Horizons, Mystery Weekly Magazine, Lavender Review, and other journals and anthologies. Schraeder's nonfiction has appeared in Vastarien, Radical Teacher, the Intellectual Freedom blog, and other places. Awarded first place in Crystal Lake Publishing's 2021 Poetry Contest, Schraeder was also semi-finalist in Headmistress Press' 2019 Charlotte Mew Contest. Schraeder believes in ghosts, magic, and dogs and writes about not quite real worlds.

For the last 15+ years, **Ali Seay** has written professionally under a pen name. Now she's shaken off her disguise to write as herself in the genre she loves the most. Ali lives in Baltimore with her family. Her greatest desire is to own a vintage Airstream and hit the road. Her novella *Go Down Hard* was released in 2020 by Grindhouse Press. For more information, visit aliseay.com or find her on twitter @AliSeay11 or Instagram @introvert_fitness

B. J. Thrower is experiencing a career resurgence, selling/publishing twelve new fiction stories the past two years, including a s&s novelette upcoming in Weirdbook #49. Half of a mother/daughter writing duo, she's previously published in Asimov's and many others. A SFWA member, she's the 2021 VP of OSFW (Oklahoma Science Fiction Writers). Find her on Facebook or her website: bjthrower.osfw.online

Karen Thrower is a native Oklahoman, wife, and mother. She holds a Bachelor's Degree in Deaf Education from the University of Tulsa. She's also a member of Oklahoma Science Fiction Writers, serving as the Facebook "Wizard." Her works are on Amazon at: amazon.com/author/karenthrower

Victory Witherkeigh is a female Filipino author originally from Los Angeles, CA and currently living in the Las Vegas area. Victory was a finalist for Killer Nashville's 2020 Claymore Award, an Honoree for Cinnamon Press' 2020 Literature Award, and Wingless Dreamer's 2020 Overcoming Fear Short Story award. Her work has appeared in both online and print literary magazines and genre fiction publications of horror and dark fantasy. She has her print publications in a horror anthology, *Supernatural Drabbles of Dread*, and a literary short story in *Overcoming Fear* through Macabre Ladies Publishing and Wingless Dreamers. Read more at victorywitherkeigh.com.

Editor's Biography

Nicole M. Wolverton was raised in the hinterlands of rural Pennsylvania and now lives just outside Philadelphia city limits in a 100-year-old house. She is the author of *The Trajectory of Dreams* (Bitingduck Press) and an active member of the Horror Writers Association. Nicole's short fiction, creative nonfiction, and essays appear in a variety of magazines and anthologies, most recently in the Saturday Evening Post and in collections from Dark Ink Books and the Hungry Ghost Project (for a full list, please visit www.nicolewolverton.com). She holds a B.A. in English from Temple University and is in the midst of earning a master's degree from the University of Pennsylvania.

When Nicole isn't facing down the forces of evil and menopause on paper, she can be found on a dragon boat, on an airplane, or appreciating gin and stinky cheese. Come say hello on twitter @nicolewolverton.

TRIGGER WARNINGS

The following list isn't exhaustive, but it takes into account certain themes and situations included in *Bodies Full of Burning*:

> Abuse (emotional/psychological)
> Anxiety
> Cancer
> Domestic abuse
> Gender dysphoria
> Loss of a child
> Loss of a parent
> Transphobia

Printed in the USA
CPSIA information can be obtained
at www.ICGtesting.com
LVHW041352080724
784914LV00002B/179

9 798536 828199